mit

Producer & International Distributor
ebookPro Publishing
www.ebook-pro.com

A Second Chance in Paris
Ziv Amit

Copyright © 2019 Ziv Amit

All rights reserved; No parts of this book may be reproduced or transmitted in any form or by any means, electronic or mechanical, including photocopying, recording, taping, or by any information retrieval system, without the permission, in writing, of the author.

Translation from the Hebrew: Maya Thomas
Contact: authorzivamit@gmail.com

ISBN: 9781655905155

A SECOND CHANCE IN PARIS

ZIV AMIT

Day One

Gate C4, Early Morning
Kate

"Here's to a wonderful vacation," I quietly say to the man walking beside me, as I walk the small step from the sleeve to the plane. He doesn't answer me and keeps walking, turning his back to me. Maybe he didn't hear, I tell myself and show my ticket stub to the air hostess standing at the entrance to the plane. "Good morning," the air hostess smiles at me. A quick good morning smile from immaculate lips painted appropriately, making sure to move on to the next passenger in line after me ever-so-professionally, not held up by the mumbling of my lips given as a reply to her.

"One mustn't be held up when smiling," I think to myself, one also mustn't ask how I am and how I'm feeling. If you were to ask, I would tell you, but there's a long line here that needs to arrive right on time, an entire row of smiles to be seated precisely in the right place, otherwise we'll get held up. So, I move forward.

I hold on to the boarding pass firmly in my left hand, as if it were an incredibly valuable certificate, and I hand it to the next air hostess. She looks at it with yet another lip-smile while automatically directing me with her hand. After all, everyone walks towards the same seats and it really doesn't matter what direction she would point to. But the truth is that I'm asking for a few more seconds to myself, a few seconds to stand in the entrance, a few seconds to breathe, a few seconds to give myself space before I sit down on the small seat next to the man everyone calls my husband.

The man everyone calls Adam or "Your Husband" and I call "The Tall One" when I'm angry at him, is walking ahead of me through the aisle and ignoring me. He's lugging his little trolley behind him, the one he carried loyally all through the duty free, and he's busy looking for our seats. Once he finds the right number he lifts the trolley over his head and crams it nonchalantly into the small overhead compartment.

"You see," The Tall One turns to me as I sit next to him, "I told you there's no need to check in a suitcase, a small bag is more than enough."

"Maybe for you, not for me."

"What do you even need to take with you?" he retorts with a disgusting and disrespectful tone. "What do you need to check in a suitcase for? Because of you we're going to have to wait for another thirty minutes till your suitcase arrives, and that's if it arrives at all and doesn't get lost along the way, because the porters' union just decided it's their breakfast break, and then we'll be starting our vacation with a fun hangout at the airport. Do you really love airports that much? How much stuff do you need to pack for five days? You women, you're all the same."

"I'm your wife, I'm not all women," I answer him and he returns to his silence. I hate it when he calls me "You Women" and not by my name, Kate. And I hate that he tries to make me feel small. For a while now he's been painfully biting me and I've been repressing, sometimes I wonder how long it'll go on for and if I'll make it to the end point, is there even an end point to rock bottom?

"Breathe slowly," I whisper to myself inaudibly while my

fingers nervously play with the fastened seat belt. I want to unfasten it but I know I'm not allowed. As it is, I feel suffocated on airplanes, feel like I'm running out of air, return to feeling alive every time a flight ends. The seat belt just adds to the feeling of suffocation, The Tall One's proximity to me does too. I always have to sit on the aisle seat and he always has to sit next to me, thus missing the view from the window and putting up with the middle seat. Eventually he'll dump me and he'll have all the view he wants. Breathe slow and deep, this thing is going to take off to your romantic vacation soon, romantic vacation, remember?

"Take off already." I look at my red nails, slitting invisible lines with them on the stiff gray seat belt strip that's pressing my stomach. "You asked the manicurist for blood-red nails especially for this vacation, you wanted to be special," I think to myself ironically. "You could have asked her for a transparent-pink or a lime-green color and it still wouldn't have mattered to him." You could have even not gone to her and he still wouldn't have noticed. As it is, lately he hasn't even looked at me.

"Are you comfortable?" I ask The Tall One.

"Yes." He replies and returns to reading the brochures crammed in the seat pocket in front of him, doesn't bother taking interest in whether I'm comfortable too. I turn to look at him, he's immersed in himself, intently reading the laminated emergency instruction sheet. Slides here and here, exits at the front and the back, in case of a crash don't panic and don't forget to take off your high heel shoes, so that you don't let all the air out. I so want him to tell me something nice and loving, but he keeps his silence.

"She's such an idiot, what was she thinking?" I overhear the conversation from the seats behind me. The scream of the engines from the plane taking off and soaring high up in the sky has ended, and I look at the land beneath us growing more distant and at the sun rising over the horizon. "I told her that's exactly what would happen if she left him and they got a divorce, why did she up and leave?" The conversation from the back seats continues to reach my ears. For some reason I already have a feeling I can guess the rest of that sentence without hearing it, as if it was taken from a crappy movie with an obvious ending. She must have gotten sick and tired of him treating her in such a disgusting and cynical way, so one day she just had enough and decided she wanted her freedom, and not only did she want freedom, she had the audacity to act against her good friends' warning, those friends who are now sitting behind me and gossiping about her. Of course, they were right, because they're playing the part of the gossiping friends and they knew in advance that he wouldn't engage in chasing her and that she'd remain alone. Now their friend is alone in the world without that nasty guy, she's aging more and more each day, she can't find another guy and she's so broken up that she couldn't bring herself to join them on the trip. They're so right, it's always fun to be right when you play the role of the onlooker.

I shut my eyes and raise a bitter smile in view of the back seat chatter, wondering to myself about the one who should have known that this is what would happen, did she really know this is what would happen? Did she think that this is what her friends would say about her after her marriage had crumbled? Did she even try to save it? Perhaps, for example, by taking the initiative to organize a romantic vacation? The kind that would revive what they once had? Maybe she decided that she wouldn't give up but didn't manage it?

"Don't listen to them." I keep my eyes shut and try to banish the woman from the back seat's gossip away from my thoughts, "You have a few hours of flight time, you don't need to fill them with thoughts about other women that you don't even know." You have yourself and you have Adam and that's an entire world in itself. I give myself a confident smile, try to empower myself, and place a hand wrapped in blood-red colored nails on Adam's thigh. He's focusing on a game he's playing on his smartphone and avoids looking deep into my eyes, just like he's been doing all through recent times.

"I don't want to give up on us," I whisper silently, mainly to myself, though I'd love for him to raise his head a bit and listen to my thoughts. But I might be whispering so silently that there's no chance he can hear it, and if he does hear me then he must be choosing to ignore it. I can take the tweezers out of the makeup bag and pinch him a little, see how he reacts, say on the ear lobe without him noticing. In the past I'd do it to him and he'd laugh and grab my arms tightly, which would end in either tickling or fucking, depending on the mood. But I think that this time it wouldn't get a warm welcome, this time I'm going to sit nicely, cross my arms and wait for the air hostess with the perfect smile to serve us breakfast. I try to shut my eyes again and relax, maybe even listen to the rest of the fascinating conversation from the back seat about the one who should have known, but I think they already suspect that I'll tell her everything they're saying about her, so they've moved on to whispering now. Or maybe they're worried that I too will up and leave just like her, but they don't know me.

"Enough already with all these thoughts, they're not leading you to good places." Be positive, try to think of all the fun you're both going to have. You booked a romantic hotel for you two, you'll be eating in awesome restaurants with waiters who smile condescendingly, you'll be walking around arm in arm together like all the tourists, you'll be taking loads of silly selfies, buying yourself pretty clothes and making love in the hotel every evening.

The noise from the engines is calming me down a bit and I manage to smile to myself optimistically. "It'll be great," I promise myself, but the lump at the bottom of my stomach, the one containing the reaction he had when I told him I'd booked us flights and a vacation, that lump isn't dissipating. "Omelet or sweet-cheese blintzes?" I hear the voice of the air hostess standing near me at the aisle, pushing the breakfast cart, maintaining a perfect smile. Can't wait for this flight to end so I can leave the plane, breathe and smile too.

Luggage Conveyor at Charles de Gaulle Airport, Morning Time

I'm making sure to keep looking at the wall in front of me, staring at a big billboard hanging on the wall, a happy couple running towards the sunset while holding drink bottles in their hands. "Will everything crumble for you guys too because of a book?" I silently ask the giant billboard, "I promise you that you'll find that special something which will ruin everything for you, even if it isn't a book, it'll definitely be something."

Of course, The Tall One was right, and we've been waiting in the luggage hall for a while now, waiting for the luggage conveyor to show a sign of life and start working. I'm making sure not to look at him and I concentrate on the ads around me, but I know he's walking back and forth at a safe distance behind me at the other side of the hall, tightly holding on to his gray trolley and feeling good about himself and also right. He's probably thinking up new sentences that he can later spout at me to make me feel small. I feel guilty as it is, will another degrading sentence or two really make a difference? Do you think this is what's going through the minds of all the women around here patiently waiting with you? What are their spouses going to blame them for?

True, I took a big suitcase, that's how I like it, I like to spend time every morning deciding what I'm going to wear. I have a pair of morning-time walking shoes, another brown pair, low-heel evening shoes - so that I'm comfortable walking on the stone pavements, gorgeous red suede boots for clubbing, if we go out. Two knitted cardigans and two sweaters, a coat, three blouses, two extra pairs of pants, two skirts, toiletries, makeup and a fishnet outfit which I brought to wear especially for you, in bed at the hotel, so that we can fuck like we used to with me on top and you full of passion.

True, I too am to blame for what happened between us,

true, it happened because of me, true, I was wrong. But I'm here with you, isn't that enough? I'm starting to understand that maybe for you it isn't enough. I can't handle this thought right now and I prefer to turn my gaze towards the static black luggage conveyor. Wish it would start working already.

You didn't even want to go on this vacation. You explained that to me a number of times, hinting slightly as well as more firmly, you didn't bother packing anything for yourself either, you just ignored my requests. If I hadn't filled your trolley the night before the flight, you'd probably have arrived at the airport with a plastic bag and a pair of underwear. You're being very romantic right now, walking around behind my back and making me feel bad about myself. If I weren't full of guilt, I'd probably give up. All I'm trying to do is fix what I've broken, trying to stop feeling guilty. Don't you make mistakes too sometimes?

The man in charge of the breakfast committee for the airport porters' union has decided I've had enough of the torturous regret at the horrible act of checking in luggage, and so now the black conveyor has started spouting out bags at a steady pace, causing a crowd of people to tightly gather around it, rejoicing and mumbling words of excitement. "Don't cry, my dearest suitcase, he's not really angry with you, it's not your fault, it's my fault, I'm the one he's angry with." Never mind, soon enough we'll get to the hotel and start this vacation.

Hotel in the Latin Quarter, Room 314, Before Noon

"What should we do now?" I ask Adam, after I finish peeing in our small hotel room's toilet. I've been holding it in for an hour and now I'm looking in the mirror again and smiling, surprising how a clean toilet can do wonders to a woman's mood.

"I don't know," he snaps at me, "You were the one who chose the romantic program, so you choose, I'm only here to decorate your conscience."

It's also surprising how fast a woman's smile can reassemble into a lump of sadness. He's probably been planning that sentence ever since I informed him of the vacation, slowly sharpening it into a fine singular arrow ready to be launched precisely at the right timing. Like a hunter who knows that justice will always be at his side and that he must end the battle with a winning strike, he kept silent and still till the moment of launch.

"You may be tall and I do love your body, but you're not just here for decorating my conscience, you're also here for communal enjoyment." I'm trying to soften the arrow's blow, it having wounded the lump in my stomach. But I think that after such a massive achievement, he's not going to give up that easily. It's been a few weeks already that he's been lugging his frustration around, and now everything's coming out and we're already here, and it's not possible to turn back time, I wonder if it's at all possible to turn back time. "You really are a little bit naïve," I whisper to myself.

"I don't feel like walking around the city, there's nothing interesting here," he continues. I know he's just saying that, it's clear to me he'll love this city just as much as I do. What have I done to deserve this?

I look at the open window of the hotel room, it's draped in dark and heavy hotel curtains. But the curtains are drawn to the sides and the city's houses are peering at me through the gray light of clouds and morning, beckoning me to them. I want to go out to her, after we had already had a little taste of her earlier when we walked over here from the metro, me with my big suitcase and him still not volunteering to help me. I'm trying to concentrate on the view of the houses from the window, thinking about whether to continue the conversation or remain silent, feeling the lump in my stomach debating with itself whether to transform into a block of indifference or to climb up to the eyes and begin accumulating into tear drops. The tears always flow out of me eventually, and when they do he always tells me that he doesn't understand what it is I'm crying about and that I'm using crying as a manipulation, I hate it when he tells me that.

I stop the argument and turn to the suitcase. It's big and it's loyal, and it satisfies all my needs. I use all my effort to lift it onto the bed, I have no desire to ask him for favours, I prefer to busy myself with dispersing its contents into the closet and the bathroom, maybe in a few minutes he'll change his mind.

"After I finish unpacking, I'll walk around our room and discover all of its secrets," I promise myself. How much is there really to discover within this room? It's charming, but it's tiny and as of right now I'm not certain that we'll manage to cram both of our egos into it, especially Adam's, which has recently inflated to alarming proportions. He's trying to stand his ground and so he takes on the observer position, as he usually does, choosing to stand by the window with his hands in his pockets, wandering with his gaze between the outdoors' inviting streets and the indoors' room containing the woman who took him on vacation. The same woman who's now busy with hanging her skirts in the little closet and organizing the sweaters on the shelf. Adam's little trolley has been left orphaned next to the front door without him touching it, and I wonder whether he's simply waiting for a moment of distraction on my part, say while I turn to the closet, so that he can run to the door, grab the trolley and run away from me and from this room. "I don't think so," I whisper silently, I think he's just enjoying his win.

"What did you say?" he asks.

"I said maybe you should bring your trolley over and give me your toiletries, so that I can put them in the bathroom, and then we can go walk around the city."

"Why did you bring us here? Do you think we fit in here?"

"Yes, very much so, loads of romance, love, cafés, we fit in."

"Yeah that's so us," he answers back with sarcasm. "We're an island of mistrust, sorry, not we, you're an island of mistrust."

"Enough with the mistrust, let's fix it, it'll be nice, we'll go look for some silly museum like the rest of the tourists," I try, but understand that with every new attempt of mine, his feeling of desire to shut himself in the room only grows.

"And that's really what you think, that museums will fix what's broken?" he asks quietly.

"Yes, museums will fix what's broken, because the thing that's broken isn't that bad and doesn't need that much fixing," I choose to answer him back.

"Of course, because you're the only one who decides when to break and when to fix, not me, I just have to agree to it."

"Then you better agree to it, because there's you and there's me and there's no more than us two in this room. We can always argue, fixing is harder."

"Yes, fixing is harder."

"Then let's do what you want to do in order to fix our broken world, what do you want to do?"

"I don't want to fix, I want to stay in this room, leave it a little bit broken, it won't make a difference."

"That's what you want? To sit in this room for the entire vacation and ruin it? What will you do in this room? Is that how you think you'll fix something? This room is nice but I'm not planning on sitting in it for our entire vacation and ruining it."

"I'm sorry that I can't act according to your pace, now I'm breaking, now I'm fixing," he tries to imitate me in a sarcastic and vicious way, "I'm not like you."

I'm running out of words a bit and I can't decide whether to continue trying to be nice to him and humiliate myself a bit more, or to give up.

"Come on, it'll be nice for us together," I offer him my hand and feel like I'm starting to repeat myself, I guess this is how it feels when you've run out of arguments.

"I'm still broken, I want to stay in this room," he repeats himself, ignoring my hand, I guess he too has now run out of arguments.

"Then you're welcome to stay in this room, see you in the evening, have a nice room-day," I spout quickly, pick up a sweater from the open suitcase on the bed, grab the key card for the room from the chest of drawers, as well as my bag and the tears that are beginning to flow out of my eyes, and I go out the door into the hallway and down to the elevator. I have to do something with myself, take myself away from here.

Boulevard Saint-Germain, Clothes Shop, End of Morning

"Do you have these pants one size smaller?" I ask the shop assistant and try to force myself to have fun. I'm not really having fun.

It was difficult for me to go down the elevator at the hotel with tears choking at my eyes. I quickly exited the lobby to the street, hiding my nose with a tissue I had in my pocket, hoping that if anyone noticed me, they'd think I was just blowing my nose. I don't exactly remember where I went to and where I walked around, I just wandered aimlessly, crossing one street of gray houses after another, ignoring the autumn trees and the scattered leaves on the sidewalk. Even the sight of the boulevard with the white houses and the little balconies which signalled to me that I'm in Paris couldn't lift my mood.

I think I was mainly waiting for a phone call from him, a message ping explaining to me that he's a nasty jerk, that he's sorry and that he's on his way to meet me, wherever I may be. A message saying he wants to search the city for me with a bouquet of flowers and a silly smile the way it once was, bring us back to who we once were. But the phone chose to be as silent as a grave, buried deep in the little bag I was carrying on my shoulder, not sending me any signs of life, and no matter how often I stopped to look at it, it wouldn't ring, nothing, silence.

"Don't succumb to him," I try to uplift my mood. Try to have fun, or at least make believe you're having fun. For example, you can go shopping for clothes. "After all, you're a woman," I smile to myself bitterly, "And what does a woman do during a time of crisis in every mediocre movie ever made? She eats ice cream in front of the TV, or starts smoking, or goes shopping." So go shopping, you like to go shopping.

"Maybe the phone's broken? Maybe it isn't getting any reception?" Put the phone in the bag and stop looking at it all the time, it'll end up breaking just from you turning it on and off over and over again. You're so ridiculous, didn't you just say you're going to go shopping and spend some money? This looks like an appropriate shop.

I'm standing in front of the mirror and trying on the clothes, they're pretty, but they're not fitting me the way I'd like them to. I really do feel like the star of a mediocre movie, trying on clothes and taking them off and not liking any of them. "If shopping doesn't work then I can always situate myself in front of the TV at the hotel and eat ice cream," I explain to myself as I exit the shop without having purchased anything and begin looking for another interesting shop. "I have to make do with shopping," I explain to myself, The Tall One has already occupied the sitting-in-front-of-the-TV-in-the-room part and hasn't left you any space next to him. I guess that's how it is in life, the one most miserable is the one who gets to sit in front of the TV with ice cream.

"Try to have fun," I walk on the sidewalk and talk to myself, "There are loads of tasty places in this city."

A Small Café in the Latin Quarter, Noon

"Come to us," the fresh pastries in the display window whisper to me. To enter or not to enter?

I'm standing at the entrance to a café that's inviting me in with its scent of freshly baked pastries, deliberating whether to go in or give up. It isn't really a crucial question, but for some reason it feels like it is for me. It feels weird for me to go in and sit down at a café alone, as if I went on vacation without a partner. I feel like if I even just cross the threshold, I'll have declared to myself that our romantic vacation has failed and has left nothing for either of us but our own individual slivers. I know that it's silly, I know it doesn't really matter, I also know that I've sat alone at cafés numerous times in the past without giving it a second thought, but still, this time seems different and I stand before the threshold hesitating.

"Come to us," the fresh pastries in the display window whisper to me, "You won't be sorry if you taste us."

"You really should," the smell from the coffee machine on the counter tells me, "I taste wonderful."

"He's not worth it, you deserve someone who'll appreciate you," the old waiter with the white apron silently smiles at me, he's cleaning the tables, wondering to himself whether I'm coming in or not.

I feel like I'm missing out by standing before the threshold like this. A woman wearing an autumn-colored dress, holding shopping bags full of new clothes, standing and assessing the café with sad eyes. Assessing the little tables which look like they were scattered around randomly, the older man reading a newspaper in the corner while his aging dog naps by his feet, the two men in dark suits who are standing at the counter and drinking a quick midday coffee on their way to a meeting, and the old waiter with the white apron who looks like he spent his entire life here.

I look at them longingly for a few minutes and then I back away. "I'll find something to snack on along the way," I comfort myself as I turn my gaze and walk away with swift strides. Even though it may be silly, I'm still not ready to let go of the feeling that I have a partner and that we're here together, I'm allowed to imagine that we'll still take a walk on the bridge while embracing each other.

The Bridge, Afternoon

There's a row of women in white dresses standing on the Alexandre III Bridge and mumbling quick words in Japanese or Chinese or some other language, and I slow down my pace for a moment and wipe away a tear. I stand in awe at one end of the bridge, looking at how it stretches from one side of the city to the other, decorated with a row of copper street-lamps with golden trimmings, which seem as though they were glamorous soldiers in formation awaiting the order to light up for the night. Tourists and pedestrians walk across it and brides posing for wedding photos add little white love stains to it.

"You're so emotional," I lovingly tell myself off and stop to look at them. They're leaning motionless against the marble rails in various positions, listening to the photographers' instructions. They look to me like big white flowers made of satin fabric, white-handed porcelain dolls with eternal smiles and immaculate makeup. Each porcelain doll has a proud partner standing at her side, holding a little bouquet of flowers in his hand, while the stately black limousines quietly wait on the side, as if they were a patient and well-mannered whale.

I too am standing on the side, making sure to keep a polite distance, unable to take my eyes off of them. They look to me like an image out of a movie that may be called Life and may be called Illusion, and I wish them a pleasant movie along with their men in black suits who are holding their hands, including the one wearing a pink dress who decided to rebel against conformity and be a different flower, "You're allowed to be a little bit different." I wish upon myself to have her pink courage.

Hunger disrupts me and I'm forced to disconnect my eyes from the white flowers as well as the pink one on the bridge and continue on my path. The pastry I ate at the airport in the morning is long gone, not having survived my wandering through the streets, and all this walking with shopping bags and aching feet is wearing me down. I can return to the hotel but that's where The Tall One is, and he may be sitting in the room and waiting to have a fight with me, so I try to delay my return as much as possible, and look for more attractions and excuses to stay outdoors.

"What about going to the museum like all the tourists do?" I debate with myself. I like to walk around in museums, stand in front of a big painting and picture myself inside it, to feel like I exist in the mind of a great artist who chose to add me to his creation. Sometimes I find myself standing like that in front of a work of art for a long time, imagining myself in a different reality. The crowd around me changes incessantly but I don't care, I focus on the painting and my imagination. But that doesn't feel right for me today, today it seems suffocating to me, caging me in silent and closed-off halls and I want air and freedom.

I feel like I've run out of all other options, and so I reluctantly start walking back towards the hotel. Even the Eiffel Tower, which peers over the city's structures, now seems distant, belonging to people who wish to experience the romantic city together. Now, with every step I take towards the hotel room I'm starting to feel the distress accumulating within me again, knowing that soon I'll be fighting with him.

"Remember," I tell myself as I walk up the hotel stairs, "there's no way you're going to miss out on the show tonight."

Hotel in the Latin Quarter, Room 314, Evening

"Is that what you're going to wear this evening?" I hear his voice from the next room and try to understand if the sound of jealousy has replaced the sound of humiliation. A tight black skirt is laid out on the bed, coupled with a semi-shiny black button-up blouse, and the red suede boots are placed by the bed, as if declaring their owner's intention of using them tonight. I'm focusing entirely on the eye-shadow which I'm carefully applying in front of the bathroom mirror, bluntly ignoring Adam who is wandering around my clothes suspiciously, around the ones carefully laid out on the bed as well as the ones drenched in today's sweat which are currently tossed in the corner of the room on the wooden chair.

He's playing the game fully by not asking me where I was and what I did, I'll give him that. And to my own credit, I'll say that I've managed to banish the feeling of guilt and I have no intention of telling him anything. I feel bad about having wandered the streets of a foreign city without him caring about me, and I have no intention of letting him revel in the knowledge that he's succeeding at making me suffer.

I'm deliberating whether to give him a little ladder so that he can climb down off his high horse, or to leave him there with that I'm-always-right feeling that he so loves to take up during every argument. "How was it at the hotel?" I ask as I start drawing a line over my left eye with my eyeliner.

Adam is ignoring my question and I can hear him turning the TV on. He's playing with the remote and zapping between channels, skipping between a local news broadcast and a foreign channel and an Australian horse race, I think maybe he should go back to playing with his smartphone, he'll probably enjoy that more.

"Are you really going to go to a cabaret show? I told you already I don't want to go there."

"A real surprise," I explain to my eyes which are looking at me through the bathroom mirror, "you asked him what he wanted to do during the vacation, he didn't want to do anything, you bought tickets to a cabaret show and now he's explaining to you that he wants to ruin that." I have a sarcastic side but I don't think I'm very good at it, I just want us to go out to one show in one club in one city, together, as a married couple. I'm not looking to be right and I'm not looking to win an argument and I'm not looking forward to going out alone, but I'm slowly realizing that that's probably what's going to happen, and that I'm going to have to decide whether to break down in tears, or to collect my lump of a self and go out.

"You're not going to give up, you're going out to the show, even if he doesn't go with you," I whisper empowering words to myself, trying to elevate myself way above reality.

"Are you really planning on going by yourself to a pervert show? Naked girls and horny men?"

"You'd be surprised, not all cabaret shows are about naked girls and horny men, cabaret was born as a wild satirical act and not as a local peep show, and you're more than welcome to join me if you'd like," I answer him as if I were a high school teacher as I squeeze into my skirt. He never used to be like this, I know he wants to go, but he also doesn't want to forgive me.

"It's not my kind of thing," he says as he wanders around

the room, looking for some space for himself without having to look at me buttoning up my blouse. The room's size, which looked warm and romantic to begin with, is now feeling tight and irritating and closing in on me, as if it doesn't have enough air for two people.

"Come with me, you'll see that you'll enjoy it, you'll see that we'll enjoy it together," I try to go near him and hug him but he recoils. "I know that deep down you do want to go, and you should, maybe you'll get to see other women's breasts," I try on my seductive tone.

"I've already heard your opinion of other women's breasts, that was enough for me," he shoots below the belt and my seductive self loses her smile and backs away from him.

"Shows like that are not my kind of thing," he repeats himself, I guess he decided to stay on his high horse and test my bravery and determination.

I'm ignoring him, so I open the little closet and stand in front of the full-length mirror that's attached to the inside of the door, tucking my blouse into my skirt and checking myself out, I like what I see, but I have a lump in my throat.

"So how was the museum today?" he breaks down and looks for something to talk about.

"I didn't get a chance to go today, I was doing other things, I'll probably go tomorrow or the next day, you're welcome to join," I smile sadly, not really believing it'll happen.

"Did you have fun at the hotel?" Maybe he managed to climb off the high horse?

"I won't have you go to a cabaret alone," he wipes away the remains of my smile.

"Great, then you're welcome to join," I corner him.

"No, I'm not going and I don't want you to go either," he's flinging chauvinism into the room, I'm trying to keep cool but I'm finding it difficult.

"I don't remember marrying a bigot who thinks he's allowed to tell me what to do," I feel myself getting red and agitated.

"I don't remember marrying someone who suspects that I cheated on her," he shoots dirty arrows at me.

"I don't remember marrying someone who gets messages from whores and buys them presents."

"Stop calling her a whore, she works with me at the office and she has a name and the present wasn't a present, I just lent her a book. I lent her one book, that was all, one book," he's really pissed off now.

"A book? And that was it? Just one book?"

"So, she misunderstood me and sent me some stuff, so what?"

"Some stuff? Some stuff? You mean some photos and messages and a few more interesting stuff. I don't care what her name is, the way I see it any woman who sends stuff like that to my husband is a whore and it's a shame you're defending her and not our marriage, I already apologized once and I'm not doing it again," I'm furious.

"You never apologized, not properly," he shouts and continues, "you never apologized for suspecting me. I've been waiting for weeks, maybe she'll apologize, when will she apologize, will she apologize. But no, it's beneath you to apologize, you're above apologizing," he says with a degrading and angry tone.

"OK then, so I'm apologizing now, I'm sorry, I'm sorry, I'm sorry. I'm sorry that I suspected you for having something going on with that whore, sorry, that whore from your work, I'm sorry I organized this vacation because I felt wrong for suspecting you, I'm officially sorry. I'm sorry," I answer him, full of rage.

"It's too late already."

"Too late for what?"

"Too late to apologize."

"Are you coming to the show?" I feel like he's starting to exhaust me with his mantras.

"It's not my kind of thing."

"Of course, it's not your kind of thing, your kind of thing is sitting in a hotel room sulking and feeling how right you are."

"That's right, that's precisely my kind of thing and you can leave, you've left once before, you know how it's done."

"OK then, and you're a saint, right? You're never wrong?"

"Not that kind of wrong."

"Then have a nice hotel evening," I'm trying to speak without my voice trembling while zipping up my boot. The last thing I want right now is to go to the show, but I feel like I can't back out of it. I also can't stay in one room with him.

Three high-heel taps from the bed to the purse that's on the chest of drawers, three high-heel taps to the jacket that's hanging in the little closet, eight high-heel taps to the door, fifteen taps from the door shutting behind me to the elevator on the way to the street.

A Dark Street, after the Rain

"Maybe I'm making a mistake and I should go back to the hotel?" An evening-time autumn wind is blowing at me and I tightly fasten my jacket around my body, as my red boots tap on the street's paved stones. I feel that as my hands are firmly clutching the jacket against the wind, they're also holding back the lump in my throat from exploding outwards into tears.

I straighten my back as I walk, feeling like I was right, and yet feeling so bad and so alone. "This is your marriage which is falling apart, is it really worth it to fight over the right to make choices and decisions?" I ask myself. I know the answer is yes, I need to fight for my principles, but right now I'm feeling very unmarried and very lonely, walking to a cabaret show where I'm meant to have fun.

How will I be able to enjoy that kind of show? Sit alone at a table for four, with a strange couple and a bottle of champagne, look left and right with an apologetic or humiliated smile, and have such an obviously empty chair beside me. Try not to notice the men who are looking at me with a hungry stare and the women who are checking me out with despising or pitying looks. I'm definitely feeling sorry for myself right now.

I think the metro station is after the next turn.

"Maybe I should just sit at a café or go watch a movie at the cinema instead of going to the show?" I think up ideas to myself. The main thing is to pass the time, I'll sit around for a couple of hours, or a bit more, stare at the silent smartphone, it'll stare back at me, we'll have an evening of silences, me and the smartphone. Reminiscent of the recent evenings spent with Adam. Afterwards I'll return to the hotel as if I ended up going to the show, invent a story or two about the awesome show and the bare-chested dancers, and we'll go to sleep, each of us in our own virtuous corner of the mattress. Maybe that's the best solution.

"You're not doing this, you're not giving up this time. This has nothing to do with Adam, you're not giving up on yourself, as it is you already back down when you're up against him way too often and way more than he deserves," I tell myself off. Even if the show is terrible and packed full of naked girls and perverted men without any women in the audience, you're still going there.

"Not really." After all, you know yourself, you know that if the crowd at the entrance looks disgusting you'll turn around and walk away and you won't dare to go inside. "Agreed." So I sum up the options in my mind. If that happens, we'll move on to the café option. Then afterwards at the hotel I'll tell him a made-up story about how amazing it was. I actually don't feel at all like telling him anything or sharing anything with him after he hurt me like that. "Besides," I continue my supportive line of self-defence, "this is your vacation and this is your freedom and you deserve to have fun", with or without him. "I back down enough as it is, the decision of joining me or not was his, but the decision to have fun or not is mine," I recite an encouraging sentence and try to smile, even just a little smile, I deserve it, even though I don't actually believe the sentence will work.

A light drizzle starts and I tighten the jacket around my body even more, straighten my back decisively and try to walk faster towards the metro, all the while trying not to slip over the wet paved stones, I should have taken an umbrella with me.

Another four metro stations to the club and then I'll decide how much fun I'm going to have, I already need to pee.

Parisian Cabaret Club, Ladies' Room

I'm standing in the little stall, trying not to touch anything, but I have to pee and I can't hold it in anymore. "The things that an autumn chill can do to a woman's bladder," I thought to myself as I departed the tall leather sofa at the corner of the dimly lit club, stumbled over the legs of the couple sitting next to me at the table, mumbled apologetic and embarrassed words and stepped through the low lighting to the ladies' room. In the background I can hear the music in the club, the audience's laughter erupting every so often, reacting to the three dancers and the clown. Yes, even laughter is giving my bladder a hard time, even though I don't understand the language. My cheerfulness was also heightened by the two glasses of champagne that I had received. That we had received, but now it's just me so I'm allowed to drink for two, that's the rule, right? If he doesn't want to come with me then his glass of champagne is mine, same goes for the heart shaped chocolate. I quietly shut the door of my stall, plant my booted feet on the floor, lift my skirt up, and prepare to remove my pantyhose when I hear her in the stall next to mine. She's speaking quietly, I think she's on the phone, she's almost whispering and I don't understand a single word she says. Nevertheless, I try to listen and I move my ear closer to the dividing wall at a safe distance from its surface, lest I should touch it. "Idiot," I silently talk to myself, "you don't understand anything anyway, what are you eavesdropping for? And why are you being as quiet as a mouse?" But I remain motionless, half-standing and half-sitting in mid-air, my hands clutching at my pantyhose. Her conversation is becoming more audible, I think she's angry about something and I also think she's starting to cry. Her words are coming out faster and faster and seem fragmented and less clear, she occasionally blows her nose but it doesn't stop her from speaking, and she's moving her hands around creating sounds of fabrics rubbing and a metallic clink of bracelets or a necklace. I'm starting to get uncomfortable in my current position, also my pee is still waiting for its turn and I'm beginning to feel ridiculous. But the feeling of embarrassment she'll experience by suddenly realizing that there's someone next to her prevents me from moving. I always find it difficult to think of people hearing me when I'm using the ladies' room, I even get embarrassed with Adam, who has been living with me for a few years already, I'm always aware of him being outside and I come out blushing every time I think I made too much noise. What am I going to do with him now in that little hotel room? Maybe I'll use the ladies' room in the lobby? I try to quietly peel off my pantyhose, it shouldn't make any noise but I hear a masculine voice answering her and talking to her, more like kissing her, or at least that's how it sounds to me, like they're kissing.

She's still talking and getting angry and crying but there's also kissing and the sound of fabric rubbing and his fuzzy words mixing with her words and something falls on the floor, or maybe it's actually her shoe hitting something, and I think I hear something unzipping and mixed ambiguous sounds of fabrics and a slam on the wall and she's breathing heavily and I hold my breath.

I'm finding this difficult, my muscles are starting to hurt from the uncomfortable position and my feet are aching from the boots, the heels aren't that high but they're heels nonetheless, I'm out of options and I have to decide whether to sit or to lean on something, and I'm grossed out and I support myself with my hand against the wall and oh the pee, I need to pee so badly.

Their voices are getting louder, I imagine him leaning her against the wall and penetrating her or touching her with his fingers and I imagine her caressing him, breathing heavier and faster and making these little wailing sounds like a cat. I would die if I made sounds like that, but I don't think she cares. He's whispering words I don't understand that sound like he's excited by her and she suddenly gives one major wail and then just breathes heavily, and he's breathing heavily and I hear them slamming into the wall, grabbing at something or at each other and he's groaning and speaking strong blunts words at her, and she's just breathing and suddenly silence and breaths. Breaths and the sound of fabric and a zipper and mumbling and a door shutting quietly and I'm shaking from the effort of not moving, my hand leaning on the disgusting black wall. Disgusted as well as turned on, I'm definitely turned on, I feel it in my underwear, but also disgusted at the thought of my hand touching that wall.

I breathe in slowly, allowing them to leave the ladies' room and leave my mind. I lean and finally pull my pantyhose down to my knees and I crouch, hoping no one comes in.

I'm done and I come out and shut the stall door quietly behind me, turn around to the sink and for a moment I feel like I want to die. The couple from the stall, at least I think it's the couple from the stall, is standing in the ladies' room by the sinks. She's with her back to me, looking into the mirror with her hands behind her, tucking her white blouse into her black leather skirt, and he's leaning against the wall looking at her. When he notices me, he turns to look at me and smiles politely. I turn bright red, and I'm already preparing to quickly get out with my head down and escape to the cabaret hall or India, whichever is closest, when the guy turns to me, invites me with a polite hand gesture to wash my hands in the sink, and moves away to the side wall to make room for me.

His partner, or his girlfriend, or his whatever, turns to me for a second, gives me a quick smile and returns to fixing her bra and her blouse buttons in front of the mirror. As if the fact I was in the stall next to them while she was making those sounds has nothing to do with her. I slowly and hesitantly go to the sink next to her and turn on the faucet, making sure to look straight into the mirror as I wash my hands and praying that the spotlight above the sink isn't revealing how red and embarrassed I am. I try to refrain from sneaking glances at the woman who is standing a few inches away from me. She's busy fixing her lipstick, she passes the dipped brush over her lips back and forth and when she's done, she puts it away and presses her lips together with a satisfied look. Another moment of embarrassment on my part coupled with hidden glances and I see how she leans down and stuffs the lipstick and brush into her boot, fixes it with her fingers until she's comfortable, and rises back up. The woman parts company from me with a smile and goes over to her partner, who has been waiting for her on the side of the dimly lit room, and they turn to leave and vanish, not before the guy sends me a smile and slightly bows his head at me. I've been washing my hands rigorously this entire time, trying not to follow them with my eyes, just trying to stare ahead, staring at my blushing self through the mirror, but eventually not controlling myself and looking.

I go back to the cabaret hall, cram inside the little alcove back to my seat, mumble another apology at the couple who are sharing the table with me and are having to move their legs aside again while I push myself onto my seat, aware of my pantyhose brushing against their legs and thinking that they're probably wondering why I was away for such a long time in the ladies' room. There's a muscular acrobat on stage wearing blue tights with white stars, he's flinging around a bare-chested dancer with a golden smile to the sounds of the music and the crowd's cheering and I'm making sure to look at the stage, careful not to let my eyes wander to the crowd sitting on the dark leather sofas, worried that I might stumble upon that guy's smiling look or see the woman. The acrobat in tights and the dancer are taking a bow to the sound of applause and all I can think about right now is why I don't have red lipstick in my boot, in case I need it.

Hotel Hallway, Silent and Still

It's late at night. I come out of the elevator and step out into the hallway quietly, not in a rush, thinking about the sounds and the applause and the cat. The sound of my heels is swallowed by the smoky pink wall-to-wall carpet, the night's tranquillity and the closed doors along the hallway remain undisturbed. For a moment I stand in front of our room's door and take a deep breath in, wondering what's waiting for me when I open it. Is Adam waiting for me, am I at the starting point of a new fight and blame-fest? I don't think I have the strength for another fight. I just want us to feel good together, I'm even willing to make it up to him for having spent the whole day in the room, even though it was his choice.

I'd like him to apologize for the way he's behaved since our arrival here, I'd like him to wait for me with a smile, even without flowers, a smile would be better. I'd like him to tell me he's really sorry and that he was worried sick the whole time I was gone, that he wandered the streets looking for me and couldn't find the way to the club, that he was scared that I was kidnapped and raped by horny men and now he's so happy to see me and he loves me so much and from this moment on we'll have a wonderful vacation. Anything but another fight, and silences. I take a deep breath in, get the key card out and open the door.

To my surprise the room is almost entirely dark. I see Adam's silhouette asleep on the bed, lit by the TV screen showing a golf tournament. I shut the door, not bothering with keeping quiet. I kind of want him awake, worrying about me, caring about me, not about golf. Maybe some drunken taxi driver had taken me to the woods in order to rape me, and now I'm trying to escape from him? Or maybe I was robbed and am now lying dead in some street? Or maybe I met some aging millionaire at the cabaret who made me an offer I couldn't refuse? The only thing Adam has to offer me when I return on my own is a dark room and a golf tournament on TV?

"There won't be a fight here tonight," I tell the little white golf ball as it rolls slowly towards its hole on the TV screen, "nor will there be any wild sex or some version of rekindled love." I sit on the bed, hoping my moving of the mattress will wake Adam up, but he keeps sleeping and doesn't move even as I lean to unzip my boots and free my tired feet from this whole night and from the walk back to the hotel.

I'm standing in front of the bathroom mirror, wiping makeup off my eyes and lips with a wet wipe, I love putting lipstick on at the beginning of the night and feeling the excitement of what's to come, but at the end of the night, the lipstick that's left over seems a lot closer to reality, imperfect with remnants of red shine. I straighten my back and imitate the movements of the woman who stood next to me in the ladies' room. Hand movements of fixing the bra and blouse buttons as if you're the only one existing in the world after fucking, and there's no woman next to you washing her hands and looking at you.

I'm aroused by getting into her character, I wonder what it's like to fuck in the ladies' room like that, go into a stall hand in hand with a man, shut the door and let him undress me or open his zipper with my fingers. It seems so filthy and disgusting to me, fucking like that in a public restroom, or even caressing another man or letting him touch me like that, no way could I do that, it disgusts me. But the thought arouses me more and more and for a moment I run my fingers over my skirt and underwear, imagining it's a leather skirt, like the one that the woman from the ladies' room had on. Why don't you and I ever do wild things like that? I want what she had. I want you to smile at me politely after you fuck me, I want you to smile politely at the whole world after you fuck me, I want you to fuck me and afterwards hold me tightly.

Now I'm actually jealous of the woman from the ladies' room and it's a little bit ridiculous. "You don't really know her and you're not even sure it was really her, maybe it's just your imagination?" I tell the mirror. Maybe her life is crappy and that ladies' room fuck is the boldest thing she's ever done, and she's actually a really boring woman who works at a bakery selling chocolate cakes from morning till night? At least there are similarities between us, my life is crappy too and I too want to fix my blouse. I could maybe do it in a sparkling clean ladies' room that was never used and was built especially for me, that is, if only Adam had cared about me and had been waiting for me, worried that I may have been kidnapped or raped, not asleep in front of the golf on TV.

It's difficult for me to fall asleep on a strange bed, the room is totally dark and the curtains are dark too, the kind that are made especially for hotels and prevent the yellow light of the street from penetrating in. What if there's suddenly a fire and I'll have to escape through the dark and unfamiliar room? The blanket is different too, I'm not used to sleeping with a wool blanket covered by a sheet, and Adam lying next to me also seems unfamiliar all of a sudden. The room is small and the mattress is small and he's only a touch away from me and yet seems so far away, maybe I should put on the fishnet outfit that I purchased online especially for us? The one with the holes in all the places that usually don't have holes. I can wear it and sit on him, that could be a great way to end an era of sulking and start the process of making up. The couple's voices are still wandering around my mind and I do want to, but it seems like he's sleeping so deeply that if I try to wake him up he'll only get more upset. Sorry, fishnet outfit, your performance will commence tomorrow morning.

I try to be quiet, press my legs tightly together and sleep, but the people and sounds from the club are wandering through my mind, a mixture of lights and applause, dancers with exposed breasts and one woman's wailing. I'm quietly lying in the darkness and I'm wide awake, looking up at the black ceiling and unable to fall asleep.

Day Two

Hotel, Room 314, Bathroom, Early Morning

I feel weird putting on the fishnet outfit and going to wake him up with caresses. The whole idea of waking him up with a sexy outfit suddenly seems inappropriate to me. As if I'm a character in a story about someone who's standing in the bathroom of a little hotel, looking at herself in the mirror, and looking for some courage to go wake up a man with caresses. "What exactly were you thinking when you ordered this outfit online?" I ask the stranger standing in front of me on the other side of the mirror. She's wearing a shiny black fishnet leotard which is covering my stomach, which I dislike, but is totally exposing my breasts and ends at the bottom with two thin straps, which are pressing on my lips and don't really feel comfortable. "You should have ordered one size bigger," I tell the woman facing me, as I lean down and try to lengthen the straps as much as possible. "What about lipstick? Shall we add red lipstick to the outfit?" I ask myself, "are you crazy? He'll get a heart attack from you waking him up like this." But I can't resist.

I'm not at all certain that he deserves to have me wrapped in this sexy outfit, especially after his disgusting words last night before the cabaret, but I promised myself I'd make it up to him for my behavior and I plan to keep that promise. I admit that when I planned the trip it seemed like an arousing idea, and now it's looking more and more like a bad plan that I should maybe just give up on. "It was a good idea then and it's a good idea now, he'll love it," I continue with my self-persuasion, "I think," I add hesitantly, hoping real badly that Adam will be excited by my surprise.

I can still change my mind, take this outfit off and bundle it up into a little ball, forgotten for eternity at the bottom of the suitcase. Or throw it into the trash can and have the hotel housekeeper pick it up and wear it tonight for her man. I can clean off the lipstick and go back to bed, cover myself with the uncomfortable blanket and sleep for the rest of the morning, I can still change my mind. "I won't back out," I answer myself, "I want to surprise him and I want to fix what I broke." And as a last minute thing I add the high heels which are placed by the closet and I get under the blanket. Dressed in a shiny outfit, high heels and lipstick, my hands look to caress Adam's body as he sleeps.

His body is warm against my hands, which are cold after having been in the bathroom for so long, and he moves a little bit as I start to caress him. A sliver of this morning's gray light penetrates through the dark curtain which I earlier moved in order to see the waking city, and I look at my fingers moving over his shoulder. His back is turned to me and I press myself against it, the shiny cloth of my outfit is separating us and my breasts press against him as my hands travel over his stomach and downwards. He slowly wakes up, sends his hand back and tries to grab hold of my waist, caress me. "This is blessed progress, the grumpy man is softening," I whisper and press onto him tighter. The grumpy man is also starting to get hard from my fingers stroking him, and I smile to myself in the gray light enveloping us. My red lips press against him, kissing and licking his back and his shoulders. "You see," I silently say to the skeptical woman from the mirror earlier, "I told you this has a good chance of succeeding." His hand is stretched back to feel me while my fingers caress him and I feel him getting harder under my touch. He frees himself from my grip and turns to me so that we lie face to face. I feel his manhood pressing against my stomach, rubbing against the outfit on my body, silently telling me he's enjoying the contact. Our legs wrap around each other's as we press ourselves closer together, and his feet touch the high heels I had added for the occasion. I feel his hands enveloping me and holding me against him tightly, slowly running down my back. I try to twist myself closer to him but suddenly I feel him stopping.

I get my body closer to him, looking to pull him closer to me, but his hands withdraw from me and it's just his erection which remains hard and pressed against my stomach. He stops and freezes, as if he desired me and then changed his mind. I try to pull him closer to me and kiss him. "What is this?" he whispers to me, "what is this outfit?" "It's for you, my tall man," I whisper back as I kiss his motionless lips, "a surprise from me to you."

"That's the surprise you had for me? A whore's outfit? Is that what you saw at the cabaret last night and decided to get for me? Is that why you went there? I don't want these sort of whore surprises from you."

I freeze, my hands freeze, my breath freezes, my high heels freeze and I slowly release my hands which have been wrapped around him, I disconnect my body from his, pull the blanket off me and walk over to the bathroom. I toss away my high heels on the way there, peel off the outfit and throw it into the bathroom trash can, maybe the housekeeper will want to wear it one day for her man. I get into the shower under the harsh stream of boiling hot water and start scrubbing myself with soap, scrubbing my lips from the remains of the lipstick, scrubbing my tears, scrubbing my injured pride, I sit on the shower floor, crying and scrubbing.

Hotel, Dining Room, Later

One croissant for breakfast, one piece of toast, a little bit of jam on the corner of the white plate, a latte from the coffee machine, one bag of sweetener and a piano placed at the corner of the dining room for decoration. The hostess asks for my room number and I gesture towards The Tall One with my head. He's sitting at a table with his back to me, sipping his coffee in front of a painting on the wall depicting dancers with their legs up showing their garter belts and men in top hats at a cabaret club. "How ironic," I think to myself as I look at the painting and slowly walk towards the table.

He didn't wait for me earlier. When I got out of the shower with the towel wrapped around my body the room was empty, just the way it was when I went in to shower, the blanket crumpled on the bed, the lights out, the closet door open exposing my hanging clothes and the high heels tossed on the floor. The curtain was drawn, letting in the light of the waking city. For a moment I wondered to myself whether he had packed up his things and left for good, but his trolley was still at the side of the closet, open and neat, waiting for someone to make use of it. I got dressed silently, trying to think clearly and not succeeding.

"So, what's next?" I mumble to myself as I get closer to him with my little breakfast plate, "here's a dilemma for you." One table and four chairs, I don't want to sit in front of him so that I don't have to look into his eyes and I don't want to sit next to him so that I don't accidently touch him. What I really want is for him to get up and leave and vanish, but I settle on sitting in front of him and concentrating on my croissant, taking small bites and staring at the little plate.

We're sitting in front of each other and eating in silence and I'm wondering if this is the end. I'm surprised by the fact that yesterday I thought that I'd eventually blow up at him and ruin the romantic holiday, and now it actually seems like the romance is ending with the sound of silence, without any unnecessary dramas. I have no strength left for trying to save anything, and the humiliation is too harsh for me. I wonder when the end would have arrived if I hadn't booked this romantic holiday, if I hadn't tried, if I hadn't suspected him, if I hadn't felt the need to make it up to him, why do I even feel the need to make it up to him?

The Tall One is drinking his coffee in silence, not looking at me, concentrating on the shapes that the coffee is leaving along the sides of the cup. "Maybe he's trying to figure out the future," I think cynically, "I wonder if it's the near future of a few minutes away, or the distant future of what used to be his and mine." Around us the dining room is filled with quiet breakfast voices and sounds of porcelain plates, but the silence between us is weighing me down and I'm starting to get tired of it. The Tall One finishes his coffee or his fortune-telling which seem like the same thing to me, looks up at me and says, "You were wrong for surprising me like that."

"What?" I ask him, refusing to believe what I just heard.

"You shouldn't have surprised me like that with that outfit and that morning sex, that was wrong of you," he repeats himself like a broken record.

"Wrong of me?" I'm trying to keep my cool and refrain from throwing the breakfast table at him, though I think it would only do him good.

"Yes wrong of you, I'm not OK with that, suddenly you decide I'm not right for you so you up and leave for a few days, then you decide I am actually right for you, so you come back, then you decide to book a vacation without asking me, then you decide to walk around all day without me, then you decide to go to the cabaret show alone, but then that doesn't suit you either so you come back to the hotel and get into bed with me, everything goes according to what you decide and what suits you."

I'm stunned, I don't know what to say to him.

For a moment he's quiet and withdrawn, staring at his coffee silently, and then he continues to talk while staring intensely at the coffee cup he's holding, not looking me in the eyes. "You leave you come back, whatever suits you, leave again, come back again, it may suit you, but it doesn't suit me, you don't suit me, I don't want to live like this."

"What did you say?" I ask in order to buy some time, digest what he just said, give him time to apologize.

"It doesn't suit me, you don't suit me, I don't want to live like this," he repeats himself, making it clear to me that he doesn't want me.

I wait for a moment, digesting what was just said. I gently place my coffee cup at the center of the little white saucer, look at him and say, "I'll see you in three days on the flight back." I grab my bag which was placed on the chair beside me, rise from my seat and leave the hotel, giving a little smile on the way to the hostess standing at the entrance to the dining room. What's left at the table is a quiet Tall One, croissant crumbs and half a cup of coffee.

Hotel, Dining Room, Earlier
Adam

This coffee is too bitter for me, maybe I should go and add another spoon of sugar. I've been sitting here alone at breakfast for half an hour already, with a painting stuck in front of my face, waiting for her to finish her shower and come down here.

What exactly did she think was going to happen? That she would go out without me in the evening, come back in the middle of the night, and then we'd have sex in the morning and that's it? Everything would go back to the way it was before?

It doesn't suit her to be with me at the hotel so she ups and leaves? She's behaving the same way now as she did then. Suddenly she decided that I was cheating on her, excuse me, that she suspected me of cheating on her, so she up and left, just like that, up and left. After a few days she decided it's alright, so she came back, and now it's the same thing, what does she think, that I'm some doll she can play with?

Suddenly she's into surprises? A surprise romantic vacation, surprisingly ups and leaves, surprise sex. She wants to surprise me? Maybe she should ask me if I even want to be surprised, she definitely surprised me with that outfit earlier. Majorly surprised.

She only thinks about herself, she doesn't really care about my feelings and my needs, or about whether I was hurt and maybe in need of some time to come back to her. She came back, so everything's OK. What does she think, that I'm some toy that she can emotionally manipulate? Turn on and off on a whim because now it suits her? "OK, I apologized, that's it, case closed." It's not closed for me, totally not closed, and I'm going to tell her that, if she'll be so kind as to finally come down for breakfast. Her games don't suit me at all. I won't have it like this anymore.

I wonder if Kate's planning on coming down here at all or if she'll continue showering till the evening and finish the entire supply of hot water at the hotel just like she does at home, I've had enough of waiting for her.

The Right Bank, Le Marais, Café Kate

"Are you waiting for someone?"

"No, I'm on my own," I'm finding it hard to say those words.

I'm at a small café that I happened across, a single table to myself, two chairs, facing each other.

Other tables spread around, large open windows revealing

the busy street.

I hang my bag on the armrest, place the smartphone on the table so that it faces me, I sit down and look at it.

I look up, I don't feel like I belong here. I look down at the floor, black-and-white checkered tiles all the way to the outside noise of the street, a few youngsters sitting at the tables outside the café talking with loud voices which penetrate indoors but I don't understand what they're talking about, a young couple next to me, busy with each other.

I look at my blood-red nails, imbed them hard into my palm until it too turns red, I push them in harder, feeling the pain, I look at my hand getting more and more red and I don't let go.

"What would the lady like to order?"

"Coffee, espresso please."

The smartphone is so black and quiet, I lift it up, play with it, turn it and place it back on the table, lift it up again and place it down again.

I feel a tear rolling from my eye followed by another one and another one, rolling down my cheek, to my neck. I'm thinking that they're probably messing up the makeup I put on this morning in front of the bathroom mirror, before I went downstairs to the dining room. Want to stop them but can't.

"There you go," the waiter carefully places the coffee down.

"Thank you." I look at the waiter for a moment and then return to look at the table, he has a look of embarrassment, he doesn't quite know what to do with himself and he stays standing there for a few seconds, as if deliberating whether to say something to cheer me up, or to go on with his work as if nothing happened, or to maybe go call someone for help.

"Miss?"

I look up at him, seeing him hazily through the tears. I wipe my eyes with my hand and try to smile at him, he smiles at me embarrassedly and runs off back to his work.

"What could he do with a crying woman?" I pity myself.

I get my little black mirror and a tissue out of my bag, wipe my face and look at my swollen teary eyes, the makeup is runny and ruined. I wipe my face hard, get a light colored lipstick out and apply it on my lips through the little mirror, but the tears keep rolling and interrupt my sight.

A waitress or a supervisor walks up to me, places a little plate with two smiley-faced cookies in front of me on the table, one cookie is dark and the other is cream colored. Then she places a caressing hand on the back of my neck, leans over to me and whispers words of comfort in a language that I don't understand but with softness and warmth which I do understand.

The smartphone remains black and quiet in front of me, no apologetic message from him, cutting my heart like a knife.

I pay and go out to the street.

Street, Pharmacy
Kate

I've been walking the streets for hours, I think I may have lost track of time and may have lost my sanity too, crossing street after street at a fast pace. I think that soon I may reach the edge of this city and I might just keep walking, maybe I should start walking back, check where I am. "It was very impressive, the way you got up and left him at the hotel this morning." I praise myself for having kept cool, but that was hours ago and right now I'm mainly focusing on trying to stop the tears from occasionally bursting out.

"It was wrong of me to surprise him?" That's all he had to say? That it was wrong? That it was wrong of me to surprise him with a romantic vacation? That it was wrong of me to surprise him with a sexy outfit? I think it was wrong of me to marry him altogether, why did I marry him? "The defendant is found guilty of stupidity." Stupidity and naivety at the hope that he could ever change anything about himself, and trying too hard, the defendant is also guilty of trying too hard. I always try to fix and to improve, I'm guilty of that too, oh, and also guilty of wearing a whore's outfit, because obviously I'm a whore who wants to seduce other people, like my husband for example, I'm going to turn here and look for something to eat.

I really am guilty of trying to seduce my husband. That woman from his office who sent him an affectionate selfie with a cleavage down to her knees, thanking him profusely for the book he got her and telling him how excited she was when she discovered what he had left for her inside it, she's not a whore, she's OK, there was a false accusation there. But you, the one who accidently discovered the message, you're the whore, because you wore a fishnet outfit with holes, you're the seductive over-trying idiot whore. The one who always tries to make sure everything's OK and make everything pleasant for him and where is there something to eat around here?

For all I care he can call that whore from his work, or message her saying, "My wife is acting up, come and comfort me, oh and I have loads of books to give you," and then she can get what she wants, she can have him. She can even come over and wear that fishnet outfit for him, the whore. He can take it out of the trash can and present it wrapped in cellophane to her when she rings his hotel room doorbell, that is if the housekeeper hasn't already taken it. He's probably been sitting in the room all day feeling sorry for himself, and the housekeeper probably hasn't even been in. She'll never get that outfit, the whore, I'll shred it up into tiny little pieces. How did she allow herself to fall for him and come on to him like that?

And why didn't he tell me that she was coming on to him? I would have personally taken care of her. Pull her cleavage up to her forehead. My feet are killing me, these shoes are meant to be comfortable, but I think their time is up. I would have messaged her saying, "Hello whore, this is his wife, please don't mess with The Tall One's life, he's already taken and we'll work on our issues by ourselves, no need for any assistance from whores." I need a pharmacy so I can get insoles for my aching feet, it's all because of last night's boots, though they really are terrific boots. Where is there a pharmacy around here? We would have tried to work out our issues together. And why is he trying to justify the one with the cleavage? How dare she arrive at work with cleavage like that? Is that her goal in life? To seduce my husband? Well now he's all hers. He can transfer all of his anger over to her, as well as his righteousness. She'll get a tall angry man who's always right and I'll get my freedom, excellent deal, I win. Where do they keep the Band-Aids around here? They always hide them in far away corners. Will these insoles fit? I'll take two types, the gel ones and the plain ones, and I'll take the Band-Aids with the drawings on them.

Maybe I shouldn't have gone to the cabaret on my own? Maybe I should have stayed at the hotel with him and talked things out? He must have gotten insulted by my leaving him like that after having spent the day apart. Why would he get insulted? You offered him to join you, right? It's been three weeks already that he's been saying "no" to everything you offer him, so he gets insulted because you left him at the hotel for the night? If anyone should be getting insulted it should be me, insulted by the attitude I got from him, and by him preferring to watch golf on TV instead of going out to a cool club with me. Lipstick, do you think they sell liquid lipstick here like the one she had? It doesn't matter how much I tried and how much I apologized, he's sticking with the role of the accuser, it's more comfortable for him. Does this red suit me? Isn't it too light? I'll try a darker one, is that better? Isn't it too shiny? It's definitely bold, it'll fit perfectly into my boot.

Why do I assume that I can fix anything and everything? Maybe there are things that should be allowed to get ruined, even if it hurts? Maybe I should let him live with himself in front of the TV? I'm definitely not going to let him ruin my vacation, my romantic vacation, with or without him. Condoms, I need condoms. Are you insane? What do you need condoms for? Do you want to fuck someone else? Have you lost your mind? Do you even remember how to use condoms? As if before you got with The Tall One you had dozens of partners and you jumped into bed with a different man each night. I really was surprised that Adam chose me, I'm really small and not that pretty, I always knew there were better looking girls than me, but he chose me. Ribbed or smooth? What difference does it make? As if you'll actually use them, I can pick smooth ones with a cherry flavor, they sound like gum and I'm really hungry already. I'll have fun on this vacation with or without him, even though I'm really small and not that pretty and I felt so proud when he chose me. Where do I pay here? I want out, I need some air.

The Bridge, in the Afternoon Air
Kate

"Run away, get away from here, jump off the bridge to the river beneath it, run for your lives, don't do it," I shout thoughts in my head as I pass by the boulevard of brides leaning on white rails. They're listening to the photographers' instructions and ignoring my insights, and I want to run in between them and spread them all over the place. I wish they would spread their wings, like the white gulls flying over the river, wish that they'd take off and fly away from the photographers who are making them pose in front of the sunset, away from the grooms standing at their sides dressed in black. "Don't believe the smile, look at the darkness, when the sunset ends the night falls," I shout in my mind, "it's fraud, it's the smile of passion's death."

But I stay put, I don't have the guts to get up and shoo them away, kill their dreams and stain their white dresses with the dirt of life. What was she thinking, the bride who chose to get married in a pink dress? Is she a cream cake? Doesn't she know that white gets dirtier better? I don't even want to talk about the one who chose red, do you really think that because you chose an inflated red dress then your marriage will symbolize passion? Red, according to the ancient ones, actually symbolizes the red in your husband's eyes as he tries to make you feel small, while you're there trying to save your marriage. I have to run there and pull at their dresses, they have to listen to me, maybe they'll grow wings and fly away from here and leave me on my own with this bridge, I don't want to be alone.

Enough with the stupid tears already, keep this up and you'll eventually dehydrate and they'll find you all shriveled up and dead at the bottom of the bridge, you're not going to be alone. Did you forget about the cherry-flavored condoms that you have, the ones that you have no idea what to do with? So what if you had a really long period of time alone before you met The Tall One and you totally hated it, this doesn't mean you'll go back to being alone, if he wants to leave then he can leave, you don't need him and you'll be just fine without him. On the contrary, let him wait for you in the hotel room, let him worry about you, let him think that you found another tall man and you're currently lying in some dusty attic on a squeaky iron bed, making love like there's no tomorrow.

It would be nice to make him a little bit jealous, but what's the point if he's not calling and not looking for me and not caring about me at all? You, my not-so-young lady, are delusional. "The small crying woman sitting on the marble stairs at the side of the bridge is kindly requested to exit her life-movie." It's a crap movie, and right now, as she looks over to the whipped-cream brides in their white dresses, she starts crying on cue. Do you think they know that their romance will someday end with tears of humiliation and pain? Listen to your life-movie's director already, you're better off without The Tall One.

Hotel, Room 314
Adam

I'm better off now that she left, I'm better off without her, I don't need her driving me crazy all the time with the "I'm leaving you, I'm coming back to you." I can sit in this hotel all day long, sit and wait for the flight back.

I wonder where she is, she's been gone since this morning and it's already afternoon, she probably decided to walk around the city and get a little bit more offended by me. So what if I hurt her, as if she didn't hurt me even more before that. She hurt me a lot more when she left me that time, I think I'm starting to get used to her leaving me.

How could she just decide that I'm cheating on her like that? How could she not believe me? So what if she saw what that woman from work sent me, why didn't she believe me?

And what's the time now? I've been sitting in front of this TV since morning, why do they show such boring programs here? I have a headache, where is there a pharmacy around here? She would probably have managed to find a pharmacy around here within five minutes. Of course, she knows everything, she even knew to decide that I cheated on her. I have to find a pharmacy, the hotel reception should be able to tell me where a nearby one is.

So what if she apologized, so she ended up apologizing, so that's it? Everything's erased now? If that's the case then I can wait around for a few months too before I apologize, no problem. I have to go out and look for a pharmacy, my head's exploding, but what if she returns in the meantime and I'm not here, so then she thinks I left her?

Let her think that, maybe it's better that way, it's not like she's out there walking around and thinking about me while she's having fun in the city.

Paris 2nd Arrondissement, Resting on a Bench
Kate

"May I offer you a cigarette?" Her question startles me out of my thoughts as I sit on the bench and I smile at her politely. At least I think that's what she's asking me, as she turns to me holding out an open pack of cigarettes. I answer her in English saying "no thank you," and she replies by laughing.

I discovered this bench when I ran out of all the tears and all the thoughts. I found myself dragging my way back, trying to delay my entrance to the hotel as much as possible, stepping slowly on my aching and Band-Aid covered feet, Band-Aids with softening gel as well as ones with Donald Duck drawings. I've been walking around the city since morning, and the afternoon hours have already given way to the dark streets of evening time and end of day.

Actually, before the bench, I discovered the party. I was walking through a quiet little street, the kind that's lit with sepia street lamps which cast shadows on house doors and windows, creating shapes of light and shadow and dark silhouettes of people walking at a fast pace. I was walking slowly, enveloped in self-pity, when suddenly sounds of noise made me raise my gaze upwards, towards the square windows with the pulled-down window blinds and the little balconies wrapped in curly iron rails, and it was there I saw the party.

Three young women were standing on one of the little balconies, holding cigarettes and glasses of drinks and resting their arms on the metal rails. They looked dark against the light that came from behind them, as if they were shadow puppets in a show created solely for me. I stood in the middle of the desolate street, stretching my neck upwards and looking curiously towards the source of the noise and light.

I didn't want to keep walking, they had something that enticed me, the swishing of bracelets, the flickering lights of the cigarettes they had in their hands, the sparkling glitter of the glasses of drink, sounds of laughter which I couldn't understand, and even just the light coming from the apartment and the party sounds that came from behind the women. If someone were to watch this from the side they would probably smile to themselves, or grab a camera and take a photo. A single woman standing out on the street, lit by street lamps, looking upwards and staying completely still. This same woman was also aware of her aching feet and was searching for a bench to sit on, only for a few minutes.

"Thank you very much," my feet transmitted to me with gratitude as I sat on the bench on the other side of the street, "we did a lot of walking today." But I ignored my feet and concentrated on the party upstairs, trying to guess what it was they were talking about, what was it that was making them look so happy, which one of them was in love and excitedly telling the others about her passion using hand gestures and laughter, and which one of them was just listening. I was trying to remember what I was like at parties when I was their age, before I met Adam.

I wondered which bench I would have sat on today had I not met him at that party. I liked him from the first moment I laid eyes on him. I navigated myself through all the other women - who were much prettier than me - until I got to a strategic position from which I could send him just the right smile at just the right time, and it worked. It worked so well in fact that a few years later there I was sitting alone on a bench without Adam by my side, giving my feet a few moments of rest and staring longingly at an unfamiliar party on the third floor of a strange city.

Staring at the party and also noticing that there was someone else standing near the bench. She was standing at a safe distance from it, as if deciding whether or not she could sit down next to me. I'll admit that I was a little bit pissed off by her desire to infiltrate my private benchial territory.

"May I offer you a cigarette?" she asks me as she sits down and we begin talking.

We mainly remain silent, she's silent and smoking and I'm silent and occasionally look up at the party and occasionally sneak a glance at her. One thing is certain, she's beautiful, so beautiful, absolutely stunning. Not that kind of cold thin beauty you see with models who have already forgotten what it's like to smile, but a deep and quiet beauty which is amazing in my opinion, and it's not that I'm into girls, not at all, but she's simply beautiful. I return to looking up at the party and at the silhouettes on the balcony, feeling jealous of their exchanges of cigarette sparkles and gossip, and searching for a reason to speak to the beauty who's sitting next to me on the bench.

"Are you with the party?" I ask.

"Yes," she replies and smiles, I think she too is pleased at the chance to talk.

"Then why aren't you going upstairs?" I ask, wondering whether I've just crossed the line of appropriate politeness.

"I feel fine right here."

Two or three minutes of silence pass by, I feel like we're both looking to continue the conversation and then she adds, "I'm waiting for my boyfriend, he should be here soon, we made up to meet here."

I smile at her.

"I don't feel comfortable going upstairs by myself, I like it when we arrive as a couple."

"It's nice to arrive at a party as a couple."

"Do you have a partner?"

It's a little bit difficult for me to handle that question right now. Not to mention the fact that I'm not sure I currently know the answer to this seemingly simple question.

"No, I don't, I did."

"Never mind, someone else will take his place," she smiles at me.

For a moment I really feel like smoking, I've not smoked in years, I used to smoke, not a lot and I quit, the smell that would stick to my hair and the clothes in my closet and wouldn't go away bothered me. Then I occasionally smoked at parties, but I quit that too and now I'm suddenly feeling the urge for a cigarette, just one.

I ask her for a cigarette and she takes one out for both of us, I get closer to the lighter she's holding, her hands shelter the flame from the breeze, and I stay sitting closer to her. We both smoke silently and look upwards, she's deep in her thoughts and I'm getting reacquainted with the taste of smoke in my mouth, wondering why she's not calling to see why her boyfriend is running late, but too shy to ask, it's none of my business anyway.

"He's a photographer, my boyfriend," she says after a while, without my asking.

"He's shooting some model right now and he doesn't like it when I interrupt him with phone calls, so I'm waiting."

"With me," I tell her and smile.

Suddenly she turns and faces me and says, "I haven't introduced myself." We shake hands with an amusing formality considering we've already shared a cigarette and we introduce ourselves to each other, but the only thing on my mind, as I look at her and smile, is what a beauty she is.

She looks at her phone as if she's expecting something from it, I too want to look at my phone, which has remained silent for such a long time, but I'm worried that she might ask more questions, so I resist it. I don't want her boyfriend to arrive now, I don't want her to go up to the party with him and leave me on my own to find my way back to the hotel.

"Maybe you'd like to come up to the party with me?"

"What about your boyfriend? Don't you want to wait for him?"

"He's been delayed for a while now, come on, join me, it'll be fun for you."

I really want to join her and go upstairs, but I'm worried she's offering this out of politeness and I'm looking for excuses to turn her down, I don't want to be the poor little reject who was found on the street wandering aimlessly, the one people talk about behind her back without her knowing. In fact, there's no need to talk behind my back, I wouldn't understand anyway.

"I'm after a whole day of walking around in the city and I'm not dressed for a party."

For a moment I worry that she'll accept my excuse and give up politely, but to my delight she doesn't.

"Come on, I'm embarrassed to go upstairs alone, join me, there's loads of artists up there who think they're really something, but they're not, they definitely don't know how to dress, come on, it'll be fun for you."

I fake deliberation for a moment longer and then accept

her offer with a smile, and we go to the intercom by the front door. I have a strong feeling of not belonging, not to the party and not to the hotel that awaits me, and as for her, I have no idea what she's thinking about as she takes me in, a stranger off the street. We climb the spiral staircase together to the third floor, to the party.

The Party
Kate

"He usually tends to sleep with the girls he shoots, combining photography and sex with each one of them, that's what it's like when you're a famous photographer," the tall man next to me whispers gossip in my ear. He's chaperoning me at the party and he tells me this as he notices me looking at the photographer and the impressive model who just walked in. The photographer loudly greets everyone with hugs, while the impressive model places her hand in a small yet territorial gesture on his arm. My chaperone thinks I'm looking at the couple who walked in, but I'm actually concentrating on the almost-invisible movement of humiliation and pain across The Beauty's face, seeing how she slightly shrinks and walks over to greet the photographer with a hug and a kiss, shaking the model's hand politely.

"She's a well-known model," the man next to me adds some more information as he gets a little bit closer to me and is obviously feeling a little bit more comfortable, he doesn't understand that it's The Beauty who has my attention. I verbalize agreement and express unimportant words of awe, but deep inside I think that though she may be the perfect model, with the right legs and the right height and the right posture and the right ice-cold smile, she still can't be compared to The Beauty, who I personally find so much more charming.

It's taken me a while to get comfortable at the party and I'm still not entirely feeling at home here, "you really aren't at home," I smile to myself. Earlier, we walked around the apartment's rooms, me and The Beauty, her arm resting on mine accompanying me, whispering people's names to me and occasionally hugging people who know her, introducing me to them as if I were an important guest from a faraway land. The music was pleasant and not too loud, so people could talk without shouting. One of the rooms had some people dancing, concentrating on themselves or their partners, embracing and moving to the rhythm. I could see the women from the balcony from across the room, this time not as silhouettes, they were wearing colorful clothes, silver, gold, black. I smiled at them as if they were old acquaintances, but they were too preoccupied with themselves to notice me. I wanted to join them, I wanted to be one of them and to partake in their joyous shadow party, but I was too shy, so I let The Beauty continue to lead me through the party, holding onto me as if I were a precious and valuable trinket supporting her.

A tall man holding two glasses of drinks approached us from the other side of the room. He's tall, I thought to myself, but totally not like my Adam, I still think of him as my Adam, I actually don't know at all if he's still mine. The Beauty introduced me to the new tall man and he seemed impressed as he handed us the glasses of drinks. He told me that he's a painter and he's currently in the process of preparing a new exhibition, and it felt to me like he was interested in me as his muse, at least for tonight and preferably in the bedroom. The Beauty found him less interesting, she continued to hold onto my arm, only half listening to him, her eyes constantly wandering towards the hallway that led to the apartment and the front door.

Now, when the front door opens and the photographer walks in, holding onto the model by his side, introducing her as if she were a shiny new toy he has just purchased, The Beauty lets go of my arm and walks over to them, leaving me to be chaperoned by the local tall man. He proceeds to give me his commentary on the characters who have just entered the apartment and then offers to dance, I'm much more interested in looking at The Beauty and the photographer but I feel uncomfortable turning him down, so I lose sight of them and let him take me to the room where the people are dancing, he places his arm around my waist in a territorial gesture and I show no resistance.

I'm finding it hard to move to the beat of the music with another man, I'm too familiar with my own man's movements and this physical discrepancy seems strange and mechanical to me. He's trying to get closer to me and embrace me, but it feels wrong and uncomfortable to me and I make sure to keep a safe dancing distance from him, creating a private bubble of music and steps for myself, closing my eyes and dropping my head back, or looking at a random point in the room, protected from him and from his ever-searching closeness. The new tall man is trying to look into my eyes, trying to create more intimacy to allow him to close in on his bedroom fantasy for the coming night, but I keep my distance and after a little while longer of dancing together I withdraw from him, explain that my feet hurt and walk over to rest on a little armchair in the corner of the room. He tries to accompany me and stands next to me chivalrously, but he doesn't really have enough space next to me and he kind of resembles a lampshade which has been lamely forgotten in the corner, standing still with no one having any need for him, surely not me. After a few moments of me ignoring him he turns away and goes to get a drink for another muse, someone else for him to try to tempt into bed tonight with drinks, dancing and conversations about art and paintings.

My eyes follow him with gratitude and I turn my look to the photographer and The Beauty who is by his side. They're standing in the center of the room, the photographer's head almost swallowed whole within the flowing locks of hair of all the women surrounding him. He's standing there wearing dark jeans and a black shirt, surrounded by women wearing dresses and tiny skirts, as if he were a dark and menacing stain enveloped by twinkling stars. He's using animated hand gestures to describe some work of art while everyone's eyes look up at him admiringly. The Beauty has her arm around his waist, as if she's trying to keep him all to herself, but he doesn't strike me as the all-to-herself type. I see his eyes, how they smilingly wander around, I see his gaze rolling over each and every one of the women surrounding him, making sure they're his. And the women retort with excited smiles at his words and with random touches on his arm, completely ignoring The Beauty's presence.

I look at The Beauty who's still holding on to the photographer, hanging onto his arm and ignoring how his eyes wander across all the women who are clinging to him. She's trying to maintain ownership over him, though I think she doesn't stand a chance against the attack of the surrounding dresses and touching hands. I find her interesting and I like her and I feel bad for her, it's not easy to live with that sort of relationship. "Your imagination is working overtime," I tell myself off, "you know her for half an hour and already you feel sorry for her and her sad life story." Perhaps all the stories you tell yourself are actually one big make-believe? Maybe he's actually the most faithful man in the world? Maybe they actually have a wonderful relationship and he's actually very sensitive and listens to her every night before bed way more than your Tall One does? How can you know what they have going between them? Whatever the case may be, my imagination seems much more interesting, and besides, she looks sad and I like her.

"I wonder if I could live that way with my Tall One," I continue with my line of thought. Live with the knowledge that every so often he picks up someone for a night or two of adventures, while you're there admiring him and loving him enough to stay instead of leaving him. "Me? I saw what that woman sent to his smartphone and I freaked out and accused him of cheating, there's no way I'd agree to that kind of free-lifestyle arrangement," I laugh to myself.

"It would be interesting to know how he's doing, do you think he's still waiting for you at the hotel?" I wonder as I check my smartphone, which looks like its usual dead self. Nothing, not even a hint of interest, maybe something happened to him? Maybe I should call him to make sure he's alive? Just a tiny little sign. "Are you insane? Don't you dare, have you forgotten what happened to you this morning?" You're not calling anybody, he definitely has a reason for not calling you and it's definitely not a reason that's in your favor, if he cared about you he would have called by now and if he's lying dead in some street then he deserves it. Enough already with your delusion of love and relationship maintenance, you're at a party, so sit down and have fun. But not with that local tall man, I really don't like him, and put the smartphone back in the bag, you're not making any phone calls, you don't care whether he's gone out or stayed at the hotel.

Hotel, Room 314
Adam

"What's the time? Where am I? At the hotel? Where is Kate? Did she call?" I think I slept a lot and it's taking me time now to wake up and realize where I am. I have no idea what I did all day, at least my headache's gone, I don't think I did anything today.

My watch is placed on the bedside table and I check the time, it's evening already. I spent a whole day inside the hotel room, what a terrible day.

"You found a great way to spend your vacation, closing yourself off in a dark room at a hotel with the curtains drawn." Maybe I should keep this up for another day or two, make it a real great vacation.

"I hurt her." I sit on the edge of the bed, place my head between my hands, rub my face and try to organize my thoughts, I don't exactly know what to do with all of them. That's absolutely not true, I just can't admit to myself that I was mean to her. That I've been mean to her this whole time.

"I've been mean, I've been really mean." I look at the carpeted floor of the room and rub the back of my neck hard. Maybe I'll turn the TV on for a bit? I can't get myself to tell her that, to say, "I've been mean to you." I think I'm better off looking for something to watch on TV than dealing with all these thoughts. What kind of husband am I if I can't admit this sort of thing?

"Is that what you want to do? Run away from her and escape into the TV?" I ask myself, but I know that if I admit it I'll have to apologize to her or try to fix things. She definitely expects me to apologize, she's my wife, I know her, I know she expects me to apologize. I'm sorry, but I can't apologize. She hurt me so bad, it was so painful.

"So apologize, so what?" I can't, not after she accused me of cheating on her like that. What did I do that was so bad? I just gave someone from work a book to read, that's where it all started. Later on, when it got all complicated, I tried to explain to The Little One what had happened and she refused to listen to me or to believe me, she just up and left. I like calling her The Little One, ever since I first laid eyes on her I thought of her as The Little One, my woman, standing among them all and catching my attention with that wonderful smile. How can I forgive her for leaving me like that?

"But she's making an effort." Yes, that's true, she is making an effort and I'm conversing with my thoughts and trying to understand what it is I should do. Maybe I should retreat back to the TV, I'm not sure I can handle everything that's happened.

I know she's sorry and I know she's trying, but it doesn't seem like it's enough for me, it's only enough until her freedom comes into the picture. Yesterday when I told her I didn't want her to go she just up and left, what should I have done? Stand there crying and tell her she broke my heart when she left me that time? I really did cry when she left me that time, she doesn't even know that. I'll never tell her.

How can I even apologize? Where can she even be? It's late already.

"Maybe call her and find out where she is?"

I don't think I should call her, what can I tell her after my awful behavior this morning?

"You have to do something."

Not right now, I'll wait, where could she be? It's really late.

At the Party, Really Late
Kate

The music is quiet now and the apartment is almost empty, hardly any people left, most have already gone. It's taking me a moment to look around and remember where I am, I think I napped in the little armchair in the corner and now I'm slowly waking up. Two couples are still slow dancing in the other room, and a few people are sitting and talking or just embracing or napping like I just did. People are still scattered around the house, but most of the guests have already left, taking with them the sounds of commotion and leaving nothing but faint mumbles of conversation. "I shouldn't have had alcohol here, that was too much considering the day I had," I think to myself, I must have been an interesting topic of conversation sleeping here the way I did while the party kept happening around me, "the poor little reject off the street with nowhere to sleep, what are we going to do about her tonight?" The thought makes me blush and I hope no one notices.

I sit in the little armchair for a few moments longer, looking around, letting my body wake up, thinking it's the right time to get out and continue the journey to the hotel.

On my way out I glance through the open balcony window, it's vacant and empty, as if inviting me over, and I walk over to the curly iron handrail decorated with metallic filigree, grab hold of it and look down at the street beneath me.

I look down, searching for my bench, searching for my silhouette which was standing alone in the street earlier, looking up. The street is desolate now and there's no one to take my place down there, nothing but dark sidewalks and yellow lights of street lamps casting shadows, and the occasional person walking swiftly by wrapped in a coat.

I have no desire to return to the hotel, but I think I've taken advantage of this party's hospitality to the max, especially after having fallen asleep the way I did. "Time to return home,

Cinderella, your glass slippers are already hurting you and tomorrow you have a brand new day of wandering the streets," I convince myself sullenly while I take the smartphone out of my bag, it's still silent and lacking any messages. Adam is still insisting on not calling, I'm thinking that maybe I should have given the local tall man another chance, even though I didn't really like him and the thought of his bed gave me a slight feeling of disgust. At least I have the hotel's address so I can return there easily, with the memory of a nice place where I spent the past evening.

I wander over to the front door while surveying the third-floor apartment one last time. The two couples dancing slowly, each couple holding one another tightly, the couple standing near the kitchen counter, him caressing her breasts and her moaning, and the empty balcony visible through the open window, delivering an autumn breeze into the apartment. I spot the photographer and The Beauty together on a couch in the corner, half sitting, half lying down, this time on their own. The pack of groupies has dispersed, and The Beauty is celebrating her victory for tonight under the photographer's caressing hands.

A few steps, a little wave of the hand, a smile and an inaudible "thank you" while I make my way to the front door, The Beauty smiles at me and waves goodbye. A split second later she jumps up towards me, grabs my hand and pulls me over to where they're sitting, "Come on, I'll introduce you to him."

"You're very pretty," the photographer tells me as he stands up to shake my hand. The compliment makes me smile. I'm not really pretty, I'll never be, but I always feel nice when I'm told I am. I definitely don't come anywhere close to the beautiful woman at his side, or to the perfect models who cackled around him earlier. "Come here, join us, my Beauty told me about you," he adds, and even though it's already late and I don't know if the offer is made out of politeness alone, I'm looking for excuses not to return to the hotel, so I sit with them.

The Beauty situates herself comfortably on the couch while taking her shoes off and tossing them on the floor. She raises her legs onto the couch's fabric, places her hand on the photographer's shoulder, and gently caresses his neck with her fingers. The sleeve of her dress is pulled up a little bit and I notice a tattoo of a name written in a cursive font on her inner arm, I think she's got the photographer's name tattooed on her arm, but I'm not sure.

"I heard you like to look in on parties from the street," the photographer tells me.

"Only when your Beauty sits next to me and keeps me company."

They both laugh and he places his hand on The Beauty's thigh. His fingers slide a little bit upwards under her dress, becoming enveloped beneath the colorful fabric. He notices me looking, but he doesn't seem to mind, The Beauty doesn't seem to mind either, she places her arm around the back of his neck.

"And what do you enjoy doing during your vacation?"

Fight with my maybe-ex-husband, let him ruin our vacation, wander around aimlessly all day, crash strangers' parties.

"Walk around the streets a little bit, sit at cafés, a little bit of shopping, museums, all the same boring things that all tourists do during their vacations."

"You came to our party, so you're already a little bit less of a tourist, you're already a little bit more of a local."

Yes, and I also went to a cabaret show on my own which is definitely not something most tourists do, and I also heard a couple fucking in the ladies' room which definitely makes me half local, and I almost threw a few brides off a bridge - brides who came here especially from faraway lands so they could get married in a romantic location - which is probably something that all locals do here at least once a week, and now that I'm noticing your fingers caressing The Beauty and noticing her enjoying it, I'm definitely a local.

I keep my thoughts to myself but not my smile, so I smile to them in response.

"You're very pretty, have you ever been photographed?"

I'm finding it difficult to deal with this sentence. On the one hand, it's so banal and corny, and I've heard it so many times from so many men, men who obviously held cameras in their hands solely to get women like myself into bed, which makes me want to puke. On the other hand, according to the amount of models floating around him earlier, he seems to be a pretty famous photographer, or well-known, or something big in the industry. And there's also The Beauty, who I'm fond of, and I don't know how she feels about questions like that one and I'd like to know. I look at her in search of an answer, but she just smiles at me, either that or she's getting pleasure by the photographer's fingers hidden under her dress.

"I don't think I'm pretty," I answer him while thinking

about how strange this scenario is, though there's something about it that I like.

"You're pretty, I think you're pretty, I'd like to shoot you."

"And who do you usually shoot?" I divert the conversation away from the embarrassing subject of my prettiness.

"I usually shoot people, strong and powerful photos," he describes his photos by gesturing with his other hand. His way of expressing himself impresses me, he looks to me like someone who's immersed in his own life, living in a parallel universe of fantasies and creativity. I've never been photographed like that and there's something very flattering about it, but I don't really suppose that he's serious about me, especially considering he's surrounded by much better options than me. I wonder what Adam would have to say about all this, I also wonder why he hasn't looked for me yet, he probably wrote that whore from his work that his wife left him and so could she just pop by for a little bit of comfort, she better not.

"I've never been photographed like that, by a professional photographer, I imagine it's very embarrassing."

"Of course it's embarrassing, that's what I look for in my photography, the embarrassment, the emotion, not the immaculate photo, but that moment expressed through the eyes. It's not challenging to be a model who's willing to do anything for success, the challenge is to find the emotion, the real people."

I'm trying to think of the meaning of what he just said and I'm unsure, with the late hour and the alcohol that was consumed it's a little bit difficult for me to understand precisely what he means. And what was that about willing to do anything?

"The models, it's their job," he continues without my asking, "they're great on camera, I get paid for it, they get paid for it, it gets published later, the photos are perfect. But, you see, people who don't do it as a job are the best subjects to shoot in my opinion, because they bring their own uniqueness to it." He's speaking solely to me, looking into my eyes the way he did the entire evening to the pack of hotties who surrounded him, and I feel like I'm becoming a part of his fan club. I don't think he's actually trying to impress me, I feel like he's blasé to the women who meander around him, giving little or no importance to whether they desire him or not. "It's not really difficult to trick someone like me," I advocate myself, what's someone like me added to his collection going to do for him? There's just the small matter of The Beauty at his side, as well as the small matter of my marriage, to the one who really should just call and apologize already, or drop dead.

"And which real people do you usually shoot?"

"I meet them here and there, it's not a regular thing, people who seem special to me, interesting, who have a fascinating story behind their gaze, those are the ones I offer to shoot."

"Then I'm interesting, not pretty?" I accept my fate in this world, if you only knew how interesting my story really is. I think my story's at my hotel room as we speak.

"That's not what I said," he smiles at me.

I keep quiet and smile back at him embarrassedly. I feel so pathetic, but there's something so enticing about the way he gets excited by art and creativity.

"The person I'm most interested in shooting is my Beauty, and she's not a model," he adds as his hand climbs a little bit further up under her dress, she in turn looks away from me, gently kisses his cheek, and returns to look at me with a smile. I think he's making her feel really good.

"She really is special," I think to myself and look into her eyes. This entire scenario seems real strange to me, I'd like to know how many more women have already been in this situation with these two. I don't actually think that I'm the first or the last one, I'm better off being realistic and not allowing myself to fall into any delusions of thinking I'm special or something.

"And do you shoot The Beauty often?" I turn the subject over to her.

"As often as I can, when we have the time and the right mood for a shoot."

I want to continue the conversation and ask him if he shoots her in the nude too, I'm curious about that, but I don't dare, so I keep quiet.

"Tomorrow morning before sunrise, we're doing a shoot by the Pont Neuf Bridge, maybe she can join us and watch?" The Beauty answers my thoughts, asking the photographer while looking at me.

"That could work," the photographer thinks for a moment, looks at The Beauty, I think he's deliberating with himself, and then turns to me and says, "Do you want to come?" He makes the invitation official and they both look at me.

I'm tired and it's already late, but the offer seems charming to me. Charming and stressing and also a little enticing, especially with the photographer's hand continuously caressing The Beauty's thigh with small strokes that I can't ignore.

"I'll probably just get in the way," I play hard to get. Don't give up on me, please.

"Not at all, it's not in the nude or anything like that, just a little bit of revealing clothing," The Beauty answers me and I'm glad she's the one doing the talking.

"If it doesn't bother you, I'll be happy to come along," I answer with a polite tone but inside I'm celebrating.

"It won't bother us at all, on the contrary, it'll be nice and you'll enjoy it, will you know how to get to the bridge?"

"I'll find the way," I promise both them and myself.

"Arrive one hour before sunrise and dress well, it will be a little bit cold, I want to shoot The Beauty before the sun rises, that's the best light for a photoshoot."

"I'll be there," I say with a smile and rise from my seat, I want to stay with them for a little while longer, I want them to take me in to their nice and touchy-feely couch, I don't want to go to The Tall One's cold hotel, but I think they want their alone-time now and I'm becoming a third wheel.

I walk over to the front door and The Beauty runs after me, grabs me tightly and whispers in my ear "do come," and with that word I march back to the hotel at this late night hour.

Hotel, Room 314, Late Night Hour
Kate

I quietly shut the door to the room behind me and try to get my eyes used to the darkness. The window facing the street has the curtains drawn almost fully, with just a narrow crevice of yellow light penetrating through their gap creating a thin line of light along the little room. I consider whether or not to turn the light on, I don't know if Adam is in the room and I don't want to wake him up if he's sleeping, on the other hand it's stupid to be feeling my way through the darkness like this if he's not even here. I eventually choose a compromise, I want to turn on a little light so I start going through all the switches, hoping the switch I choose doesn't light up the entire room.

The bathroom light spreads shadows over the room, and I now see him sleeping in bed, covered in the blanket. I wonder if he spent the whole day here in the room or if he went out to see the city, the main thing is that he's sleeping on his side of the bed and not invading my half of the mattress.

I sit myself down on the edge of the bed, trying not to rattle it too much, and quietly take my shoes off. I see him moving a little bit and I freeze, the last thing I want right now is for him to wake up. I have neither strength nor desire to hear him. I don't want him to ask me where I was, I don't want him to start looking into what I was doing, I don't even want him to decide he should apologize right now. If he wants to apologize that badly he can wait till morning, not now.

My feet ache from all of today's walking and I massage

them gently, I carefully remove the Band-Aids and look at the red skin on my heels, I lean down and slide my hand along the aching skin with a slow and tired movement, I have to buy myself new shoes.

I quickly undress and throw my clothes on the chair, all I want to do right now is crawl into bed, cover myself with the blanket and sleep, but I feel smelly from this whole day. Walking the streets, smoking that cigarette, the touch of that man who danced with me at the party which made me feel uncomfortable, the humiliation from this morning. I have to shower, I won't manage to fall asleep like this.

"Go to sleep already, you have to wake up real soon." I try to forgo the shower, lie down on my side of the bed keeping a distance from him, but even with the exhaustion I can't fall asleep, I turn from side to side and eventually give up and get up to shower. And still, even with the scent of the soap and the face cream, I can't fall asleep.

I shut my eyes and imagine the photographer's hand, climbing up and caressing The Beauty's thigh while they're talking to me. I want to be caressed that way too, out in the open, without him caring whether or not anyone's looking, his hand climbing up my thigh, making me close my eyes, making me tremble, I so miss being touched. "I could have let the local tall man play around with me a little bit," I whisper to myself, but I didn't even like him, his touch didn't feel nice and I'm not aroused at the thought of him, I need to think about someone else. "And what about the photographer? Do I want him?" I liked the photographer a lot more. There's something attractive about how his eyes stare, channeling his blasé attitude towards what others think of him, that willingness to enjoy life as it is without having to account for anything to anyone, as if only his desires exist in the world, but I don't know if he's suitable for me or not, I can't manage to decide. I don't really have to decide anything, he has The Beauty and I have the man who doesn't want me, the one sleeping with me in the same hotel room right now, so all I have left is my imagination.

I've never been in that kind of photoshoot. Do you think she'll strip in front of me when he shoots her? Outdoors in the nude like that? I don't think so, though I don't think she'd really mind being naked at a photoshoot. They didn't even talk about nudity, why am I thinking about nudity straight away? I mean, she actually said that tomorrow he's not shooting her in the nude. Would I be willing to be photographed in the nude? There's no way I'd agree to that, but it turns me on to imagine myself undressing. Will he want to shoot me tomorrow? If he asks me, I'll turn him down.

Without noticing, my hand shifts down my night shirt and starts gently caressing my nipple, pleasant movements which correlate with my thoughts. "You're definitely not going to fall asleep this way," I think to myself, but the feeling of my nails against my nipple is nice, as are my thoughts.

I lie on my back and start stroking my thigh with gentle movements the way the photographer did in front of me, imagining his hand slowly climbing upwards and imagining The Beauty's closed eyes and smiling lips, thinking about how I would feel were I in her place, but then I feel Adam turning around and my hand freezes and I hold my breath and stop the stroking.

Why do you care if he hears you? He can't hear a thing, he's sleeping like a log. If he were awake he'd probably be charging at you with allegations and wanting to know where you went and what you were up to. He can stay asleep in his corner and you can continue with your thoughts, and your stroking.

But I can no longer concentrate on The Beauty and the photographer's hand and I press my thighs tightly together, trying to fall asleep in spite of my fantasies.

Also at the Hotel, Room 314, Late Night Hour
Adam

I'm lying in bed and trying hard not to fall asleep, keep my eyes open, concentrate on the little crack between the curtains, the one allowing a narrow sliver of light to penetrate into the room, and I wait, but my eyes shut every so often and I doze off. Once in a while I pick up my watch which is on the bedside table, check the time and put it back in place.

I'm waiting for her, trying to figure out what it is she's doing and where she could be at such a late hour, maybe she actually decided to go somewhere else? But I'm mainly waiting to apologize to her, waiting to tell her I'm sorry.

I can hear the key card sliding in and the door opening and I know I should turn around and speak to her, I've got sentences and questions ready to go, but I stay lying down motionless, staring at the crack of light from the street and doing nothing, I have no courage now, I'm scared.

What can I even tell her? I don't want to fight with her, I just want to know that she's alright after everything that happened between us. "Do you really think she's alright after what you did to her this morning?" I ask myself silently. At least she came back, she's here. I want to tell her I was worried about her, but I'm scared that she won't want to listen.

I try to move a little bit, maybe she'll start a conversation. But she's not talking to me and I prefer to remain with my back to her and keep staring at the closed curtains, let her think I'm asleep. I hear her undressing. I like looking at her as she sits on her side of the bed with her back to me and undresses. Unhooks her bra and places it on the bedside table, peels off her underwear and lays it by her bra. I can imagine her doing that. The thought of her exposed back and her ass arouses me and I start feeling myself getting hard.

Kate goes into the bathroom and doesn't shut the door, she must think I'm asleep. Puts the toilet seat down and pees. She returns to the room without showering, lifts the blanket and gets into bed, doesn't touch me. I'd like her to touch me, even just a little bit, lay her hand on my back, a light gesture of contact.

She smells like cigarettes, do you think she smoked? I don't think so, she quit ages ago. Maybe she went back to smoking out of spite. That doesn't make sense, she was probably at some place where people smoked. I hate that smell, it took me ages to convince her to stop smoking. We almost broke up because of her smoking when we had just started going out, I don't think she smoked tonight.

Maybe I should turn around and tell her something? I can

apologize now, I'm sure she's waiting for that, I can pretend that I only just woke up and politely ask her where she was, and then I can say a few apologetic words, I'm sure she'd like that.

"Are you sure she'd like that?" It doesn't seem like she's trying to caress you or hug you the way she did this morning, she's not even touching you and it's not like the bed here is that enormous. Isn't this her way of hinting that you've been mean to her for a long while now? And what will I do if she refuses to forgive me? What will I do then? Take my things and leave?

Let go of these thoughts, try to get some sleep.

I can't fall asleep, I'm lying in the darkness with my eyes wide open, trying to listen to The Little One, to the sound of her movements. I hear the blanket slightly moving and I hear her breaths. Is she awake or has she fallen asleep already? I'm trying to gather up the courage to tell her I'm sorry but I can't manage to.

I hear her getting up to shower, I hear her returning to bed smelling of soap, I hear her breaths, I think she's touching herself and that turns me on, but I remain motionless this whole time, I don't have the guts to talk to her, I'm scared of messing things up.

"What now?" I think to myself. How long will you stay in bed like this, with your back turned to The Little One, full of thoughts and hard as a rock? I want her so badly right now, but I can't make the first move.

Tomorrow I'll apologize, that's the main thing, tomorrow morning everything will be alright.

Day Three

The Latin Quarter Streets
Kate

"I'm such an idiot, why didn't I ask her for her phone number?"

I don't know when it was that I finally fell asleep, I'm not even entirely sure that I managed to sleep what with all the excitement and thoughts, but morning is here and the alarm goes off. I guess I did manage to sleep after all, at least a little bit.

I quickly get up to turn the alarm off so that The Tall One doesn't wake up and start asking me questions. I walk over to the bathroom, quietly shut the door behind me and start getting myself prettied up, on the way there I go over to my open suitcase and feel around in the dark for my set of black lace underwear and matching bra, a set I brought specifically for a special occasion with my Tall One.

"He's not going to shoot you anyway," I tell my reflection in the mirror as I check that my breasts are nicely situated in my bra, and then turn to apply make up on my eyes and on a nasty pimple which grew overnight on the side of my chin. "You're just going to watch from the side," I tell myself firmly. Skirt or pants? Skirt, so you can easily change clothes if you want, and take a knitted top that you can easily remove too. Stockings? Should I pass on them or put them on? The lacey underwear will hardly be visible under them, but I'll be cold without them, I should pass on them, it won't be too bad if I get a little bit cold.

An enveloping coat, comfortable shoes, find my key card

in the darkness, grab my bag and quietly shut the door behind me, so that he doesn't wake up.

The sleepy hotel receptionist is standing behind the counter while the outside world is still dark, she gives me a secretive smile, as if I were a mistress rushing back home before dawn, or a local woman after a night spent in the arms of a gorgeous tourist.

It's still dark outside, dawn has yet to break, the street lamps are still lit and I rush towards the bridge, careful not to slip on the wet pavement stones.

"Where is that bridge? I'm such an idiot, why didn't I ask her for her phone number?" I've been wandering these little dark streets for an hour now, wrapped in my coat, searching for the bridge to no avail. Not on the streets to my right, not on the streets to my left, not straight ahead. I think I'm going around in circles.

I must have taken a wrong turn in one of the alleyways, the first one or the second one or a different one, having overly relied on my memory which has in this case proved itself less than perfect, and I've been lost ever since. "The turn to the river is at the end of this street to the right," I encourage myself and hasten my steps, but I get there and discover I was wrong again, all I see in front of me is yet another street with yet another set of street lamps.

"Why didn't I think about this? Why didn't I ask the hotel receptionist? She would have shown me the way on the map," I shout at myself with desperation and frustration after yet another street has led me nowhere. I look up and see the sky turning lighter and the night stepping aside to make room for daylight. "Do you think they'll wait for you with the photoshoot?" I ask myself hopefully, but I know it's only wishful thinking. There's no way they'll wait for me, I'll probably remain nothing but a story about the nice tourist who they had invited for a photoshoot but ended up getting cold feet. My feet really are cold right now, why didn't I wear those stockings? All I can do now is continue to search for my way, and to look with frustration at the city cleaners washing the streets in preparation for a new morning.

"Two streets on the left to the river," a passer-by points me to the right direction as he rushes on his merry way. I think that's the direction, at least he had the decency to stop and explain it to me with hand gestures included, didn't just ignore me as if he couldn't understand my question, the way a few street cleaners had done earlier when I asked for their help.

The first rays of sunlight hit the marble tiles on the Pont Neuf Bridge, coloring them yellow. The curly bronze street lamps along its spine have long been turned off, and people are swiftly crossing it on their way to work. The traffic on the roads is intensifying too. I stand at the side of the bridge, surveying it and looking for the photographer and The Beauty, but I can't spot them anywhere, for a moment I think I see them on the riverbank, but a closer look clarifies that it's in fact a homeless person who has spent the night there. I wait around for a few moments longer, surveying the area with hopeful eyes, then I turn around and start making my way back.

"No Beauty and no photographer and no photoshoot and no bridge, good morning, Cinderella," I whisper to myself sullenly as I walk back towards the hotel. I slowly walk past the cafés which are starting to open, offering a quick coffee and fresh pastries to their regular customers, the ones who stop there on their way to work. I walk and stop, making my way slowly, not in a rush to return to the hotel, gloomily pressing my nose against the front windows of cafés, staring jealously at the people drinking a quick coffee by the counters.

Another café window and another glance and another opportunity for my nose to press against the glass and another look inside a café and there they are, The Beauty and the photographer.

The Latin Quarter, Morning Time Café
Kate

The café window is making it difficult for me to look inside, even though I'm trying really hard. Two cups of coffee or tea, one plate of pastries, one photographer sitting with his back to me, one Beauty sitting in front of him and talking, one me standing outside the café not knowing what to do. It seems silly of me to go inside and join them, I definitely don't belong and I definitely had an opportunity and missed it, I also definitely want to sit with them. I'm looking for an excuse or a good icebreaker and I can't come up with anything, so I remain outside, standing and staring at them through the window. Trying to pluck up the courage to go inside, or to give up and leave, whichever comes first.

"I knew you'd make it, I was waiting for you," The Beauty

grabs my hand and pulls me after her into the warm café, having lifted her head and noticed me standing outside, she literally leaped out of her seat to take me in from the cold outdoors.

"I told you she would come," she presents me to the photographer as if I were a freshly discovered treasure, he smiles at me and politely stands up as The Beauty seats me next to her.

"I'm sorry, I got lost, I couldn't find the bridge," I try to explain.

"You're completely frozen," The Beauty holds my cold hand and ignores my apology, while the photographer waves for the waiter to come over.

"What would you like to order?" he asks me, taking on the role of the host.

A few moments later and I'm sipping hot coffee while enveloped by The Beauty's attention as she feels sorry for me, "poor dear, having to wander the streets by yourself like that." She comforts me with words, and the photographer gives me his usual warm and polite smile.

"It wasn't that bad," I answer her, "I got another tourist experience out of it, getting lost in a strange city, and besides, here we are, I found you," I try to smile and sip my coffee simultaneously.

"I'm such an idiot for not having given you my phone number," The Beauty takes responsibility and ownership, "where's your phone?" I take my silent smartphone out of my bag, hand it over to her and she quickly types in her number, "that's me," she returns the phone to me with a smile, "now you have me."

We stay silent, each one sipping their own drink, I think The Beauty is looking for my company and wants to hug me, while the photographer seems a little bit distant, though I think he's interested in photographing me and maybe even adding me to his long list of conquests. "Maybe when he saw I hadn't arrived at the photoshoot, he decided that I didn't have the potential for sex and so it would be a shame to give me any attention," I think to myself silently while pressing the cup of coffee to my lips.

"How did the photoshoot go?" I try to strike up a conversation, the silence is bothering me, though I think The Beauty is enjoying my presence even while I'm silent.

"It was fabulous, we got really sexy photos," The Beauty gets excited.

"We shot on the riverbank, he wanted to catch the sunrise in the sky with the lamps from the bridge," The Beauty takes ownership of the photoshoot while the photographer just gives his usual smile, I think he's surveying us from the side with some sort of feeling of ownership, as though he knows that if he were just to say the word, we'd both belong to him, so he'd only need to decide whether he's interested or not.

"It was really cold by the bridge for changing clothes," The Beauty continues her story, "but I wore a long dress with a slit and he hugged me really tight and that's how we did the photoshoot, it came out fabulous."

I'll admit I'm a little bit jealous of her, despite all my declarations of having no intention to be photographed. I know I'm supposed to be thinking of The Tall One sleeping endlessly at the hotel, but right now I'm just jealous of her, I'd like to be photographed like that with my body and my breasts tightly held by a sexy dress, despite the cold, it must be warming.

"It really does sound fabulous, it's a shame I wasn't there," I say with sadness.

"A real shame," The Beauty agrees with me as her hand rests on my hand, "we could have been shot together." This idea is a little bit new to me and I haven't yet made up my mind about it, so I smile at her and remain silent.

"The main thing is that you got good shots, even if I didn't get to see them."

"After this we'll be going to our apartment, to get organized and rest after the early morning start, you're welcome to join us and we can show you the photos we took," the photographer joins the conversation and I wonder precisely what he means by this invitation.

They exchange a few sentences which I can't understand and I try to decipher The Beauty's tone in order to understand her thoughts on the invitation, I'm also deliberating with myself about how I feel with the invitation, I'm unsure of both.

"Yes, come, we'd love that," The Beauty turns to me and places her hand on my thigh.

I look at them and debate with myself, their company is pleasant and interesting, though they seem like a strange couple with an unclear relationship. They have something open and enticing about them, and I really need some of that to compensate for this ruined vacation, don't I know it. On the other hand, it doesn't feel right for me to go to their apartment with them, I think that things might happen there which I'll regret in the future. There's also the issue of The Tall One who is currently asleep at the hotel, what do we even still have between us? I'm facing a dilemma.

I think to myself for a little while longer and then tell them, "I'm sorry, I have to go to the museum today, I haven't been there yet." You're such a chicken.

We sip our drinks silently, The Beauty's hand still gently resting on my thigh, and I'm unclear as to whether they're pleased with my response or not. It seems that either way, out of sheer politeness, they're not trying to convince me to change my mind. I'm a little bit sad about it, but I feel that I made the right decision.

They exchange a few more sentences which I can't understand and the photographer turns to me, "maybe you can come over for a photoshoot some other time."

"My vacation is ending soon," I answer them gloomily, they really are nice and I don't want to spend the remainder of my days here wandering the streets by myself. I'm not getting a lot of potential for mutual enjoyment during this vacation with the one who's asleep at the hotel, I wonder when he'll stop sleeping.

"That's a shame, you could get amazing photos, even though you'd probably get embarrassed," the photographer lays out a new net for me while looking into my eyes, and I kind of want to get tangled in it but I don't really have a way to, having already refused their offer, so I keep quiet and smile embarrassedly at his stares.

"Perhaps you'd like to join us this evening?"

"For a photoshoot?" I ask with a mixture of fear and hope.

"No," the photographer answers with a smile, "this evening we're going around town to shop for a few things and have a good time, we'd love you to join us." I feel The Beauty's hand lightly squeezing my thigh and I try to understand if she's hinting at something, join them? Pass on it? I look at her, hoping to get an answer.

"Come on, come with us," she looks at me with a hopeful smile, "you'll have fun, we'll show you the interesting parts of town, the sort of places that tourists don't get to see." I don't really stop to think about where it is they plan on taking me, her offer seems sincere and I like her. It also seems like a much more attractive and enticing option than walking around on my own.

We part company outside the café, a handshake and a black-eyed smile from the photographer, a hug and a whisper from The Beauty, "please come, call me later and we'll arrange it all."

The street is fully awake, flooded by the morning sounds of cars swishing past on the stone-paved roads and the commotion of people rushing to work. The couple turn towards one direction and I turn to the other, tired and smiling, as I start my search for the way back to the hotel.

Hotel, Room 314
Adam

I think it's already morning, a sliver of daytime light is penetrating through the curtains. I reach out to my watch on the bedside table and look at it, it's really late, I slept a lot. What's the weather like outside? You can never tell with these curtains.

I slowly wake up, trying to organize my thoughts, remembering last night. The Little One coming back, the smell of cigarettes, a shower, lying in bed without the courage to talk to her, trying to fall asleep and not managing it, promising myself that I'd apologize to her this morning.

"Maybe I should wait a little bit more with the apology?" I think for a moment, "you're not waiting any longer," I answer myself, "she'll end up leaving you, she'll up and leave, she'll up and leave and she won't come back the way she did that time."

"What am I even going to tell her?" I sit up in bed, looking for The Little One's sleeping silhouette next to me. I have a feeling I'm in bed alone, "where's the light switch?" I turn the bedside lamp on, I'm alone, she's gone.

"Where did Kate go? Did she leave me?" Within a second I can feel my heart pounding wildly, "Did she leave me again? How did I not hear her? She left me without saying anything?" I quickly get out of bed, draw the curtains open and look around, even in the light of day the room is lacking my Little One, there's only me, standing naked in the center of it.

"Where could she have gone? Where's her suitcase? How did I not wake up when she left?" I quickly check the room, I don't bother getting dressed, I look for her stuff, anything of hers, a sign that I haven't been abandoned yet again, I hesitantly open the closet door, her suitcase is here, at the bottom of the closet, she hasn't left me yet. I sit on her side of the bed, naked, resting from the pounding of my heart, trying to calm down.

What do I do now? And where the hell is she?

She doesn't want to see me anymore, she woke up in the morning and left.

"Maybe I can set the watch back to a couple of days ago?" Great idea, that'll definitely work. While you're at it you can ask her to wear that hot outfit again too, she'll definitely agree.

I want to keep sitting on the bed like this, naked, not do anything for yet another day, I'm not sure I can handle myself right now.

Maybe a few moments pass, maybe longer, I have no idea, but eventually I manage to get my act together and I get up and go to shower, I have to do something.

"So what? So she left, so she came back, so what? You'd think she's the first woman to ever leave you, you should thank your lucky stars that she came back, she's the first woman who wanted to come back. She's also your wife, in case you've forgotten," I talk to myself while looking in the bathroom mirror.

"I've ruined everything." That's right, you've ruined everything, now go fix it.

Maybe she's in the dining room?

Come on, get dressed already, don't miss her, don't start getting held up by all the news websites on your smartphone, she'll run off on you, get out already, go look for her in the dining room.

Don't forget the coat and the key card. She's definitely in the dining room.

Hotel, Dining Room
Adam

"Do you think she's still here?" I get closer to the dining room and wonder what I should tell the hostess at the entrance, the one who checks the room numbers. What's customary to do in these situations? Should I ask her if my wife has already gone in? Is she even still my wife? And what will she think of me if I ask that sort of question?

I give the hostess my room number and I feel tense. She smiles at me and marks something on a piece of paper which is laid out in front of her, what does that mean? Has my wife been in already or not? I don't have the guts to ask her. I survey the little dining room and the few people who are sitting in it. I don't see The Little One here, could it be that she was here earlier and has already left? Where could she have gone? Maybe she didn't even have her breakfast here?

Two pieces of bread with orange jelly, a little bit of granola and a coffee, I really need coffee. This is starting to become my regular spot, the corner table with the cabaret painting in front of it. Where could she have gone?

"It was such a great idea to wait with the apology until the morning," I think to myself bitterly, "such a great idea in fact that The Little One managed to disappear on me." I silently drink my coffee, self-absorbed, trying to think. For a while now I've been feeling a lump in my stomach, but it's grown even bigger during the past couple of days. I have a sort of feeling of continuous failure which is intensifying by the day.

"Why couldn't I have just spoken to her when she came back last night?"

"I was scared," I'd tell myself if I were being honest, but I prefer to think about where she might be instead of my fears. It's better to repress the fears, so that I don't feel weak, so that The Little One doesn't think I'm weak. This coffee's bitter, where's the sugar? I'll get some more sugar.

"Where could she have gone?" She must have gone to some museum or something touristy like that, she loves to see art, especially paintings. She always stands in front of them, stares at them with her brown eyes and gets excited. "Do you even know how many museums this city has? Are you really planning on looking for her in each and every one of them?" How will I find The Little One? I have to call her.

"Don't call her, she won't pick up."

"Why shouldn't I call her? Am I better off running around the entire city looking for her?" I can't call her, I can't get myself to call her. I won't be able to handle her not picking up, the way she didn't pick up that time, when she left me. I tried calling her again and again to try and explain and she screened my calls. And I sat on our bed feeling like I was falling apart at the seams, holding my head between my hands and whispering to myself, "she doesn't want you anymore." Are you sure you want to have another attempt at communication and maybe plummet again? Are you really able to handle that again? No, you're not calling her.

This coffee needs another spoon of sugar.

"Then what? Start searching for The Little One all over town? And what will you do if you find her?"

"I don't know." I have to try, I was mean to her, I don't know what's going to happen. Maybe I don't even deserve to find her, maybe I deserve her leaving me. Maybe she deserves someone better than me.

I'll take something sweet from the dessert cart, a little cake, I hope the elderly couple from the table across aren't feeling sorry for me.

"Stop feeling sorry for yourself, you're not a victim and you're not in need of pity, you hurt someone so you need to apologize, no one else needs to. If you don't want to call her then go look for her, but do something already. Stop it with these internal discussions and start doing something."

It's a good idea to start searching for The Little One at a museum, you can take a bouquet of flowers with you, she loves flowers.

I think it's ridiculous to go searching for a tiny woman at a museum while holding a bouquet of flowers.

It actually seems romantic, like out of some movie.

Finish your coffee already, you put way too much sugar in it, go look for flowers, there's no reason for you to go back up to the room.

Hotel, Room 314, Morning
Kate

The room is empty, clean and tidy, housekeeping was here. I toss the key card on the little table by the front door and I look around. For a moment I feel like Adam has left my life for good, he's not in the room and there's no sign of his trolley, the one which was placed by the front door up until now, as if waiting for its owner to decide what to do with it.

It takes me a few seconds to digest this and I stay motionless in one spot, it looks like this hotel room is no longer ours, as if we were never here and it's ready for new guests. Suddenly I feel a terrible panic.

"This is what you wanted, isn't it?" Maybe I should actually be feeling relieved? I quickly go to the bathroom and open the door. The glass on the sink has two toothbrushes, mine and his, two razors, pink and black, mine and his. I calm down a little bit, quickly go to the closet and open it, his little trolley is lying at the bottom, housekeeping must have put it there while tidying the room.

I sit down on the edge of the bed for a moment and breathe deeply, not before I crumple the straightened blanket a little bit, breathe a little life back into the room.

I don't know what I want. Earlier, when I was slowly walking back to the hotel, all I wanted was to sleep. I hardly slept at night, I was full of thoughts, and I had an early wakeup, so I really felt the exhaustion taking over me. All along the walk home I was trying to plan how I'd enter the room, have as short a fight as possible with The Tall One, or simply ignore him, and go straight to sleep. "No confrontations, no dramas," I told myself over and over again, but the room's emptiness has surprised me.

"Too many things are happening to me at once," I think to myself. I don't really know what to do now. I used to call up my man and talk to him, but what exactly would I talk to him about now? "Good morning, you'll never guess what happened, I got to the hotel room and it was super tidy and you weren't there. You really surprised me, where did you go?" I could even continue, "and that's not all, I'm not even sure if I miss you or if I'm finally feeling free after such a long time. What do you have to say?" What do you think? Is this a sign that you're on your own as of now? To tell you the truth, he gave you a pretty major hint yesterday morning, though I think you didn't really take it in fully. Well, you took it in a little bit.

"My Tall One, it's a shame you didn't apologize yesterday," I sit on the bed trying to think, but I'm feeling my eyes closing, "I'll rest a little bit and then we'll see," I whisper to myself as I lie down on the bed, "just for a few minutes." I take my shoes off and rest my head back, I don't bother undressing or drawing the curtains to make the room dark, I shut my eyes, just for a few minutes.

The Orsay Museum
Adam

"Of course the guard at the entrance wouldn't let me take the bouquet of flowers in with me, who brings a bouquet of flowers with them to a museum?" To tell you the truth, I didn't have the guts to walk around the city holding a bouquet of flowers, let alone stand in line for the museum with it and try to pass it through security. But I enjoy imagining doing it. I'm walking around the halls making believe that I'm holding a bouquet of flowers and that all the visitors are following me with their eyes, trying to guess who the bouquet is for, I hope she'll accept my imaginary bouquet when I find her.

I pass through the darkened halls and the paintings and the sea of visitors, clenching my fist, not to drop the flowers. I stop every so often and try to look carefully at the people in the hall, look behind me, maybe I walked by too fast and missed my woman?

"She's definitely here," I whisper to myself wishfully, deep down I know the idea of searching for her is hopeless, but deeper down I want to believe that I'll manage to find her here. "She has to be here, holding a pamphlet and looking through it like the other tourists are doing." I'm trying to concentrate on the search, but it's not easy. There are loads of tiny women here, wandering around on their own and waiting for the right man to walk over with the right bouquet, but none of them is my Little One.

After a long while I take a seat for a few minutes on a bench situated at the center of a hall, hold my head between my hands and let the thoughts rest for a bit, the breath too. A few tourists are standing in front of me, staring at a large painting hanging on the wall. Up until now I haven't looked at any of the paintings, only at the people. But I need a little rest and so I find myself looking at the painting. Two men and a woman are having a picnic in a forest. I find it strange that the men are dressed and the woman isn't, it's also strange for a woman to sit between two men, as if she can't manage to choose between them. I would have taken one of the men out of the painting and sent him off to find his own woman. Who's the artist that painted this? What did he know about love?

"What do you know about love?" I silently whisper to myself and the woman in a light suit sitting on the bench next to me looks over, trying to understand if I was talking to her. I indicate with my hand that I wasn't and I give her an apologetic look, then I put my head back between my hands and continue to stare at the painting and at the tourists passing by in front of it.

Maybe I should wait on this bench until The Little One shows up? I'll sit on the bench and look at everyone who comes near, until I see a tiny woman wearing brown shoes, standing with her back to me and looking at the painting, concentrating as if she wanted to enter the canvas and become one with it. I float through fantasies for a few moments, imagining her right in front of me so I can go and hug her, but the reality is three elderly tourists standing and taking photos.

"You have to keep looking, she's not here." I slowly rise

from the bench and continue to wander the large hallways, not before I give the painting one last glance. A tiny woman in a floral dress is standing with her back to me in front of the painting, looking at the characters in the forest, for a moment I'm filled with hope, but it's not my woman.

"I'm not giving up, I'm continuing the search," I encourage myself, despite knowing it doesn't make sense and I don't stand a chance, I'll continue on the streets and the alleyways, I want to be romantic, I want to find her so badly and apologize to her as nicely as possible. She has to be wandering around somewhere in this city, she's definitely not at the hotel.

Hotel, Room 314, Noon
Kate

The sound of a message from my smartphone startles me. I slowly sit up in the now messy bed. The room is still tidy, but I feel better when it's not overly tidy, when there's life in it. I look out the window, it's daylight outside, though it seems a few hours have passed since I went to sleep.

"Finally he's interested in my existence," I recall why I woke up and I get the smartphone out of my bag, look at it and realize The Beauty has sent me a message. I smile to myself and answer her, The Tall One isn't really interested in me and he's not bothering to message me or look for me.

The bathroom mirror presents a woman with messy hair, sheet marks on the cheek and crumpled clothes. I take off the blouse and skirt and remain standing in front of the mirror in this morning's lacey black underwear and bra, checking out the woman in front of me with relish, despite my imperfect tummy. "So I didn't really get to use you in the end," I tell my underwear and bra, "I wonder how you'd look in the photos." I grab the bra with both my hands and squeeze my breasts upwards, squishing them into round balls. I make-believe that I'm wearing a push-up bra and I raise my chin up seductively, posing in the mirror and changing positions according to an imaginary photographer's instructions. "Wait, hold on," I tell my breasts and I run barefoot to my bag which is by the front door, get the new lipstick out and return to the mirror. "Now look and concentrate," I get my face closer to the little round makeup mirror and carefully apply the shiny red lipstick on my lips, keeping an immaculate line, straighten my back and press my lips together, like the woman from the club did after she got laid.

"Well, what do you think?" I proudly ask my nipples as I stand smilingly with my back straight, "what, is the bra bothering you? You can't see? Bad bra, shame on you bra, it's not nice to get in the nipples' way," I grab the bra cups and pull my nipples out and upwards so that they stick out like little cones. "Well, can you see now? What do you think? Nice, isn't it?" I ask them and get excited by the movements of my shiny red lips. "What, you want some too? You perverted freaks, shame on you, who taught you that?" I affectionately tell my nipples off and get situated in front of the mirror again. I take the lipstick wand out and start gently painting my nipples in bright red, "I hope this lipstick comes off easily," I mumble to them, "otherwise, I think we'll have a difficult time explaining some things, I mean," I shed all responsibility off of myself, "you'll have a difficult time explaining some things."

I like the way the lipstick wand feels on my nipples and I paint them slowly, pleasured by the touch as well as seeing the two bright red erected circles sticking out of the black bra. I give myself a satisfied look and then remember something else. "Wait, we're not done yet," I tell the woman in the mirror and I run barefoot to the room, lean down into the closet, grab the red boots out and swiftly put them on.

I slowly walk back to the bathroom wearing the red boots, as if I were an erotic film star making a dramatic entrance onto a film set. I make sure to move my hips with every step, looking at myself in the mirror, grabbing my breasts roughly and moving to the sounds of an imaginary strip club song, all the while turning my body and my lips towards an imaginary photographer. Moving and dancing, changing poses in front of the mirror, smiling and making seductive sounds, enjoying my acting in front of the photographer, I'll keep doing it till he's satisfied.

"Now coffee," I tell myself with red lips.

I wait for the coffee kettle to boil and in the meantime I wander around the little room with my red boots, my miniscule lacey underwear, my black lacey bra with two bright red erupting nipples, and my blood-red lips. I make believe I'm a call girl in a thriller, waiting for the detective to come and do his job, walking back and forth in the room with perky breasts and a smile and thanking my lucky stars for the wall-to-wall carpet. "I'm so thankful for this carpet," I tell myself, without it the downstairs guests would have probably made a noise complaint and sent someone from reception over to check what's going on. "You see," I explain to my boots, "this hotel knows a thing or two about creating the right atmosphere for a thriller, they know they can't ruin a good take by knocking on the door."

The cup of coffee is warm in my hand and I don't yet want to part from the role of the call girl in the movie, I walk over to the window very slowly, after all I'm still wearing high heels and holding a cup of coffee. I like looking downstairs at the street through the window, watching the people as they rush. I recall the balcony from last night's party and smile to myself as I think about the strange scenario. I imagine myself standing here with another woman, drinking coffee and gossiping about the street below, looking at the woman who's sitting on the bench and watching us, inviting her to come upstairs. You wouldn't have actually gone upstairs were they to invite you, you wouldn't have had the guts to do so. Without The Beauty you would have ended up staying on that bench up until now, I wonder if they saw me and spoke about me yesterday.

I look at the man who's standing across the street from the hotel, waiting and checking his watch, and I'm thinking that if he only looks up he'll see me through the window, half naked and perky breasted. I like that thought and I get closer to the window, till my breasts touch the cold glass. The icy contact startles me and my nipples but I don't move back, I keep them pressed against the glass, I look at the man and send him a telepathic invitation to look up.

"I'd enjoy being photographed," I whisper to myself, this feeling of exposure arouses me. The man hasn't spotted me yet, he's looking to the side of the street and I notice a woman in a red jacket approaching him and they lightly kiss. I enjoy watching them hold hands and walk along the street, and I part company from them with a smile.

I disconnect from the cold glass window and see two round red marks smeared on the surface where my nipples had just been, and I smile to myself. "Look what you've done," I tell them off, "Now housekeeping's going to have their work cut out for them, and who knows what they might think about what happened here." Suddenly I look at the front door and wonder what would happen if The Tall One were to walk in right now and see me like this, standing in the middle of the room, dressed like a call girl from some cheap detective thriller, cup of coffee in hand and a surprised look on my face. The thought makes me laugh and I can't contain myself. "Imagine his look as he stands by the door," I laugh with my nipples, "and that's after he called me a whore yesterday morning, if he hasn't run away yet, he surely will now."

I can't stop laughing and I find myself having to put the cup of coffee down and sit on the bed, it's a pleasant laughter, liberating, cleansing, helping the body and the breath finely blend everything together.

"That's enough, now go shower," I jokingly tell off my red nipples one last time, as I take the boots off and loosen the bra clasp, tossing it on the messy bed, "a shower and then another cup of coffee."

A Café in the Latin Quarter, Afternoon
Adam

"I need a coffee." I also need a rest from all the museums. I walk past a café in the street and go in. It's a small café with an olden-day atmosphere, little round Formica tables painted red, sticking out over the black floor, reminding me of play balls.

"Coffee please." Coffee and a cheesecake and something chocolaty and tasty, I stand by the counter and choose with my eyes, point with my hand, then I walk over to a red table and place the jacket that's been hanging on my arm on a nearby chair, as if it's going to keep me company.

I was certain I'd find The Little One at the bridge by the river, she always gets so excited by wedding dresses. While I was crossing the bridge I saw them flittering about and walking around proudly, as though they were the white sails of a ship. I hastened over there, imagining her in my mind's eye standing by them, excited by the white dresses, wiping away a tear and unable to walk away. But despite having walked around through all the smiling women and the men standing at their sides, I couldn't find The Little One. Maybe she was there earlier and had already left?

"What am I going to do about not having the guts to call her?" My eyes survey the café and the waiter who's preparing my order, this entire search is hopeless. Romantic in a movie kind of way, but hopeless.

"You only prefer to look for her on foot because you don't really want to find her," the waiter tells me as he brings over the coffee and cakes, "you're just scared of rejection."

He doesn't really say that, he just looks at me and smiles politely, but I have a feeling that if he were able to read my thoughts, that's what he would tell me.

"Thank you," I tell him and smile back, wondering if he really is able to read my thoughts.

"He's right." It's hard for me to admit, but he's right, I explain to the jacket on the seat next to me. I'm scared of finding her, I'm scared of hearing what she has to say to me, I'm really scared that she won't forgive me.

"You're not thinking right," the waiter tells me as he walks over to a nearby table, "you need to buy her a present, she'll forgive you."

He doesn't really say that either, but I drink my coffee and observe the couple sitting on the other side of the café. The man is sitting with a hopeful smile in front of the woman, his hands crossed under his chin, while the woman in front of him is gently opening a little present, wrapped in green paper with yellow flowers, smiling at her man with every corner she unfolds. "The waiter's right, I have to buy her a present," I tell myself and take a bite out of the cheesecake, thinking about white flittering brides.

I return to looking at the couple, feeling like I'm jealous of them, I would have liked to sit like that at a café with my Little One, instead of the jacket that's keeping me company. "You have to get over your fear and call her," reality reminds me. I know that's what I need to do, but I can't call her. I'll look for a present for her, I'll find her after I get her a present. The kind of present like I used to get her, one that will say,

"I'm sorry I was so mean to you, I love you so much and I was heartbroken when you left me, it was difficult for me to forgive, please forgive me."

"Go already," the waiter tells me, "go and find a present for her, you still have a chance, she's waiting for you." He doesn't really say that, he's actually thanking me for my payment, and I still want to hug him with gratitude for the exchange of words we had in my mind. I go out to the street and continue wandering around the city without a specific direction, but with a specific objective, not before I look back at the café I had just left. One open present, laying on green wrapping paper with yellow flowers, and one kissing couple, sitting at a café.

Another Café, Afternoon
Kate

"I can't be late on them again," I hasten my steps, I feel so bad, I don't want to be "that foreigner who's always late and tardy." But I am a foreigner and therefore missed my metro stop, had to find the way to the other direction and got a little lost. Now I'm walking at a fast pace through all the people who are out on the street, looking at my smartphone, checking the time as well as the address of the café that The Beauty sent me.

I compare the address on my phone to the signs on the street, lifting my head to see the names written above the cafés, making sure I'm at the right place, this is the place. I'm breathless and a little bit sweaty, having walked fast with my coat on, but I managed to make it on time.

"What now?" I ask myself embarrassedly, "Should I go in?" I can't spot them on the street among all the passers-by, not even when I turn around trying to look in all directions, trying my best to look thoroughly up to the end of the street. I walk closer to the front door of the café and try to peek inside, try to see if they're there without being overly noticed and without blocking the entrance.

A few youngsters are sitting by some tables, connected by their conversation, one woman is sitting with her back to me occupied with her smartphone, two older men are sitting side by side drinking beer, and a waiter holding a white dish towel is slowly polishing glasses and placing them on the counter. They're not in there. "They're probably a little bit delayed." I'm pleased with myself for not having been late, I can calm my breath down instead of barging in on them off the street like an apologetic, breathless and sweaty tornado.

"Sorry for being late," I feel someone touching my shoulder, I turn around and lift my gaze and see the photographer standing in front of me, I smile at him embarrassedly and deliberate whether to present my hand for a shake or my cheek for a traditional kiss or maybe hug him, it seems that he too is momentarily thinking whether to hug me or make do with a handshake, and he eventually goes for a handshake and a smile. "Where's The Beauty?" I think to myself.

I try to phrase the question of why he's on his own in my mind, but he answers me before I even get to ask.

"The Beauty is running late, she asked me to come meet

you here and she'll join us shortly."

I smile at him embarrassedly, realizing that we're going to be alone, at least for a few minutes.

"Shall we go in?" he gestures with his hand and I follow him into the café, allowing him to place his arm on my waist with a light touch of ownership.

"So how have you been enjoying your vacation so far?" he asks a polite question in order to cut the awkward silence between us as we sit there waiting for our coffees and croissants to arrive. I should really stop it with all these croissants, I'll start looking like one soon. "Do you think he'll want to shoot a croissant wearing a black lacey outfit?" I let my thoughts wander and giggle to myself as I try to imagine the photographer at his studio, shooting a gigantic croissant dressed in a lacey outfit the size of a tent, with lights flashing all around them. His question takes me away from my thoughts and brings me back to the café and to the man sitting in front of me.

"What are you laughing about?" he asks and smiles.

"Just a thought I had about photoshoots," I answer him.

"What was the thought?" he asks with intrigue.

You really don't want to know, if you were to know you definitely wouldn't want to shoot me, even if I were to fall at your feet and beg you.

"I'm really enjoying myself," I divert the conversation away from his question, "I'm meeting a lot of interesting people," and I smile at him, he smiles back.

"A little bit of shopping, museums," I try to impress him and seem touristy, wouldn't want him to think that the most exciting aspect of my vacation is choosing between hanging out with them and breaking up with my husband, are we even still together?

"What did you like best at the museums?" he shows interest and trips me into the culture trap.

I think for a second, trying to extract something from my memory, I want to maintain a pleasant conversation instead of just a few moments of politeness with each other until The Beauty arrives.

"I haven't managed to go to the museums yet," I smile with embarrassment, "but I really want to, there are a few paintings I want to see and haven't yet, like 'The Luncheon on the Grass', a charming painting in my opinion."

"It really is a fabulous painting," he agrees with me, "why that one specifically?" Now he really seems interested, even though he's still a bit distant.

"Because it has something different, unbalanced, one woman with two men, she's naked and they're dressed and she doesn't care, she doesn't mind sitting like that between the two, she doesn't mind doing something forbidden," I get excited.

"Yes," he agrees with me, "a fabulous painting indeed, stirred up quite a storm in its day, the painter's courage to paint something that was seen as inappropriate." I'm enjoying talking about art like this with a stranger as we sit at a little café with quiet music, I feel as though I'm in a romantic movie and I like it. Maybe this is what I wanted when I booked this vacation for us. Am I still allowed to think of us as a couple?

"I get excited the most about artists who allowed themselves to go all the way," I continue, "artists who debated between what was allowed and what was forbidden, what was right and what was wrong."

"That's definitely the more challenging area to live in, it forces us to think about what we want, what we're prepared to do," he agrees with me, but then he turns to the waiter who's walking over with our coffee and croissants, and our conversation gets interrupted. I'm curious to hear his views and I patiently wait for the waiter to finish, but I'm too embarrassed to raise the subject again so I concentrate on my coffee cup, waiting for him to continue talking.

We eat the pastries off the little plate and I get covered by croissant crumbs. My foot is bothering me and I raise it a little bit and lean down to rub it, it's aching from three consecutive days of walking and the Band-Aids aren't really helping anymore. "Is your foot bothering you?"

"Yes," I'm forced to admit smilingly, "I walked a lot the past few days."

"Let me help you," he tells me, doesn't ask me. He brings his chair closer to mine until he's almost up against me, takes my foot and gently places it on his thigh, removes my shoe and places it on the floor. Then he proceeds to start massaging my foot with his fingers, a strong massage.

I'm surprised and not entirely sure what to do and how to react, so I stay quiet, looking around shyly. I survey the café, expecting to see horrified looks around me, but none of the clientele seem to care, not even the waiter who's busy with his own things and has his back to us. The photographer surely doesn't care, his fingers press into my aching foot. I'm trying to figure out if this is appropriate and what's going to happen in a moment when The Beauty walks in, I wouldn't want to hurt her, I think she has enough women hurting her already.

"Is this good?" he asks me.

"It's good," I answer him, "it feels good, but it is alright?" I add a question.

"Alright by who?" he asks and continues massaging.

"Alright with the café, alright with you, with The Beauty," I hesitate. Alright with my Tall One who I occasionally think about.

"With the café," he looks around and smiles at me, "it doesn't seem to me like it's bothering anyone here."

I smile with embarrassment, still, I'm a foreigner here.

"With me?" he continues to talk and returns my thoughts to his stare, "I'm fine with it, I was the one who offered it."

"And The Beauty?" I ask silently.

"The Beauty," he comes to a finish, "she likes you."

That's precisely the issue, I think to myself but I don't move my foot away from him and I let him continue, I like the way his fingers feel.

"Do you have a pen?" he suddenly asks me, while continuing to rub my foot with his fingers.

"Yes," I lean towards my bag which is leaning against the chair, get a pen out and hand it to him.

He stops rubbing my foot and grabs my hand, placing it on the round table with my palm facing up, next to the coffee cups and the empty plate with croissant crumbs. It looks like he's going to palm read my life line, or my photography and modelling line. He places his fingers over my fingers and with his other hand he puts the tip of the pen on my hand and looks at me, I look at the pen touching my skin and I look at him questioningly.

"I always write my name on a model before I shoot her," he explains to my questioning eyes with a tiger-like gaze, "that's my trademark."

I look at him and he waits.

"Should I write it?" he asks and smiles.

I deliberate for a moment, I could deliberate for days, but I think I already know what my answer is going to be.

"Write it," I answer him, unsure as to whether I chose the right answer. I wonder what The Beauty would have to say about this, I wonder what Adam would have to say about this, why does he keep coming back into my thoughts and why doesn't he apologize to me?

After he finishes, I look at his name, written on my hand in round letters. I pull my hand back and slowly run my nails over the area where the pen was, still feeling the sense of inscription on my skin from the pen's tip. I look at the red nails hovering over the letters, I look at them as if they're filmed in slow motion, as if they were the opening credits to a movie, with the café music playing in the background.

He gives me the pen and I put it back in the bag while taking my foot off of his thigh, I put my shoe back on and we continue to drink our coffee in silence. Now I'm thinking about the photoshoot, about how I'm going to be photographed in front of his smiling and inquisitive eyes, it feels unfamiliar and strange to me.

"I'm sorry for being late," I see The Beauty walk in to the

café, wearing an autumn dress, crossing the tables from the entrance towards us like leaves gently falling off the trees. The photographer gets up to greet her and they hug and kiss on the lips, his hand slides over her behind, pressing her to him. I get up to greet her and she gives me a warm embrace, whispering in my ear, "It's so great that you came," and I smile.

"Coffee?" the photographer asks her.

"Yes," she answers him while hanging her bag over the chair, and he turns to call the waiter over.

"Did you two have a nice time together?" she asks me happily when she finishes getting situated.

"Yes," I answer her, "your photographer is very nice, we talked about art and he even signed my hand," I immediately remove my fear of what would happen if I weren't to tell her and she'd notice it by herself, I wouldn't want that to happen.

"Let me see," she says cheerfully, but I'm not sure she really is pleased with his name on me. I try to look into her eyes, examine her emotions, and I can't yet decipher her, is she surprised? Offended? Angry? Happy? I'm not really certain right now.

I give her my hand and the three of us look at the pen-made signature and at her gentle pink nails moving across the ink, as though she were examining the quality and depth of the round lettering.

"Very nice," she raises her head and looks at me, "now I know you'll definitely come over for a photoshoot," she says with a triumphant smile and I smile back with relief.

Same Café, Afternoon
Kate

"Excuse me, I'll be back soon," The Beauty turns to me as she gets up from her seat and leaves the café.

Few minutes before that, we were sitting at the Café, waiting for The Beauty to get her coffee and she was interested in how my day passed since we had parted company, I started telling her and the photographer joined in the conversation.

"We're going shopping for an outfit after this, do you want to join?" he turned to me. I thought about wanting to join them, but then The Beauty told him something which I couldn't understand.

The photographer answered her and they started arguing about something that was unclear to me, but that felt like it was to do with me. The beauty spoke quietly in order not to interrupt the relaxed vibe of the café and to avoid people turning their heads to look at us, but she seemed upset and hurt while the photographer tried to calm her down. During her fast paced chatter she placed her hand on my hand, grabbing me, accidently or not, where the photographer had signed his name, and kept talking.

I sat there quietly, embarrassed, not knowing what to do. I felt that though I couldn't understand a word they were saying during this argument, it was happening because of me. Maybe it was wrong of the photographer to write his name on my hand and she got insulted by it? It seemed like that wasn't the case to begin with, but maybe I'd misread her? Maybe she didn't want me to join them on their shopping trip? Maybe she was outside earlier and had watched the photographer as he rubbed my foot? I didn't understand what was going on and I didn't know what to make of it, I found myself sitting in front of them, my hand held by hers as if it belonged to her, looking down at my almost-empty cup of coffee, praying for this argument to end, or for me to be able to politely thank them and leave.

"Excuse me, I'll be back soon," The Beauty turns to me as she gets up from her seat and leaves the café, leaving me embarrassed and him silent.

I look at the photographer questioningly, but his eyes remain on The Beauty as she leaves the café, and I don't think he's entirely aware of my presence. He only notices me when he turns back to the table, as if only just now realizing I had witnessed their confrontation.

"I'm sorry, it's nothing, just something to do with her work," he explains and I don't believe him.

"She went out to smoke, she'll be back in a minute," he continues to explain and we sit silently for a few minutes. I'm embarrassed, looking for an excuse to thank him and leave, I have no idea what he's thinking about. He's drinking what's left of his coffee and not adding any more explanations.

"Maybe I should go check on her for a moment?" I offer, trying to hide the signature on my hand with my other hand, feeling as though the letters are suddenly stinging me.

"I don't think that's necessary, she'll be back soon," he answers me and I remain seated, embarrassed, looking around the café. The people are still minding their own business, I don't think they noticed the argument that happened at the table and if they did, they're polite enough not to show it.

"On second thought, maybe you should," he says and I exhale with relief and get up from my seat.

The Beauty is standing outside the café, leaning on the building wall on the side of a bookshop and smoking, her eyes are red and I think she had been crying. I stand next to her silently, lean on the wall the same way she does, and we look at the passers-by on the street. I want her to feel that I care about her, I want her to tell me what she had cried about, I want her to tell me what they had argued about and was it because of me but I'm scared to ask, I'm scared of the answer, so I remain silent.

"May I?" I ask and point at her cigarette.

I assumed that she'd offer me a cigarette but she hands me hers, so I gently take it from between her fingers, bring it to my lips, take one drag and return it to her.

We continue standing silently and observing the street, she doesn't say anything, she just occasionally wipes her eyes with her hands and I wait, looking for something nice to say. I think about maybe going into the café for a moment and bringing her a tissue to wipe her tears and her cheeks, but I feel like my presence here is important to her and I don't want to leave her right now.

She finishes her cigarette, turns to me, hugs me and whispers in my ear, "thank you." She holds my hand and we walk back in to the café, leaving behind us the bookshop window.

Photography and Art Bookshop, Afternoon
Adam

"Excuse me, do you have books about love? I'm looking for a book about love," I turn to the saleswoman, it's hard to find bookshops nowadays, but I know The Little One loves to read and I think that this is the right place to look for her present.

"We fell in love because of a book and we broke up because of a book and I'll get her back with a book," I repeated an encouraging sentence to myself, trying to gather the courage to keep searching and not to quit. But the more I wandered through the streets, the more desperate I became and the main word I repeated was "sorry." Most of the people on the street found it difficult to understand me and what I was looking for, and mainly directed me towards newsstands, thinking I was a tourist in need of a guide book for the city. Some of the people just ignored me, or shrugged their shoulders and kept walking, as though they had already given up on love and book reading.

Eventually I succeeded in my search and I hesitantly walked in through a big door and into the bookshop, and decisively walked over to the saleswoman who was busy organizing books in the display window.

"We have photography books, you'll definitely find love there," the saleswoman answers me and points towards the relevant section. I walk over to the long display tables lit by yellow lamps and start looking through the books laid out on them, looking at the photos presented to me on the pages, thinking about one scared man who is searching for a book instead of calling and apologizing to a little woman who he loves.

"This isn't love," I think to myself as I browse through an erotic book with naked girls touching each other. Maybe it is love, but it isn't the kind of love I'm looking for. I go through book after book, nude photos, seductive poses, breasts, couples, leather outfits, I close the books and place them back on the table, I feel like I'm not in the right place.

I want to sit and think, but this shop doesn't have any chairs and it's getting late now, they'll be shutting soon and I need to make a decision. "She's going to love the same thing she used to love," I try to convince myself, but I'm not at all sure. Maybe I should try something new and get her one of the photography books laid out on the table? Maybe an erotic book with skinny women in high heels?

"And what then?" That's your present? The more scared I get about failing, the more I lose my self-confidence.

I leave the shop with the last of the customers, the saleswoman turns the lights off behind us and goes to deal with the cash register. All I got for The Little One is a book of poems, no photos and no seductive poses and no red lips and no high heels, a book of poems about love.

"Now I'm left with the real challenge, finding her." I march with the book in my jacket pocket, my hand covering and protecting it, squeezing and pushing through all the people returning from work, slowly walking down the narrow stairs of the metro station.

Metro, Early Evening
Kate

"Come with us," they try to persuade me and I am persuaded. I want to be persuaded, I don't want to continue without them.

"I'm just in your way, I should leave you two alone," I try to resist, but not properly.

"Come on, you'll have a fascinating time with us," The Beauty holds my hand tightly as though she doesn't want to let me go, "it'll be an adventure," and I pretend to debate with myself.

"We'll take you to a shop that tourists don't know about," The Beauty continues with the persuasion. "Do you think we'll find her something interesting for the photoshoot?" She turns to the photographer and I wonder what sort of outfit she's talking about, but in any case the decision has already been made internally about wanting to join them.

"I'll be happy to join you as long as I'm not in your way," I say and we leave the café and head to the metro. The Beauty is walking in the middle and smiling, one hand holding the photographer's and the other holding mine. On the way to the station she turns to me and quietly says, "what happened earlier wasn't because of you," and I smile at her with gratitude, but I don't believe her.

It's the metro rush hour and the platform is quickly filled with people returning home after their work day. They're rushing to cram into the compartments, creating a type of human wave and pushing inside before the doors close and the train continues on its way through the black tunnel.

We're standing in the center of the compartment, sardined between the people, I'm pressed between the two of them, he's much taller than me and my head is facing the knitted top he's wearing while The Beauty holds on to my shoulder, clinging to me as if she's protecting me from all the other passengers. I feel her body heat penetrating through my dress, I also feel her breasts pressing against my back. My eyes are shut and I surrender myself to their physical contact, ignoring the surrounding noises, the train's screech on the tracks, the other passengers' mumbling, the woman's voice announcing the approaching stations, the sound of the doors opening and shutting.

This feels pleasant to me, stuck between The Beauty's touch and the photographer's scent, I slowly bring my head closer to his chest until I can feel the tingling of his knitted top on my cheek and I shut my eyes again. I miss that touch so much, I haven't felt it in such a long time. Where are you? Why haven't you apologized? Why aren't you looking for me here in the metro? Do you even want me? You told me so bluntly that you don't, do you really not want me? I know the photographer isn't mine and that I'm invading foreign territory, I know he belongs to The Beauty who's holding me from behind and I'm not planning on taking him away from her. But maybe she'd be willing to let me borrow him for a while? A little loan for me to rest my head on, the way I'm doing right now, shut my eyes and not think too much.

The Beauty is holding me from behind, her arm now wrapped around my waist pressing me against her, clinging to me even more, her lips press against my hair and whisper through the crowds of people, "Do you like our city?"

"It's crowded," I answer with a smile while turning my head back and speaking quietly, so that the others can't hear us.

"We get to hug," she laughs in reply.

"I'm debating about asking you to lend me your photographer," I think to myself.

"And stand close to two charming people," I tell her.

"And become better acquainted with a charming tourist," she tells me and hugs me a little bit tighter.

"We can keep traveling like this all evening long," I laugh with her.

"But then the photographer will get jealous and we'll have to hug him too," she continues the game, enjoying the fact that she's getting me to talk , I'm enjoying it too.

"Then what shall we do?" I ask, I have a few ideas, but I think I shouldn't go beyond our game's clear rules - they offer and I accept. I'm worried that if I offer too much, they'll leave me here in the metro on my own, they have each other, I have a lonely hotel and I used to have a husband but he's disappeared.

"We're getting off at the next station," the photographer touches my shoulder and smiles at us, pausing the game and my thought process. The doors slam open and we make our way out through all the crammed people, the photographer clears the path at the front and The Beauty guards me from behind. "Come on," she excitedly grabs my hand as we climb up to the street, noticing the gray buildings and neon lights, "you'll love this street."

Pigalle District, Early Evening
Kate

We leave the metro station's white lights behind and arrive at the slowly darkening street, I look around and it's clear to me I'm not going to love this street.

The buildings are gray and covered in neon, variously colored lit signs offering sex and only sex. Sex for right now, sex just for watching, sex if you purchase clothing, sex any way you want it. Out-in-the-open sex, clearly and bluntly written on red-lit signs, sex portrayed through photos of bare-chested girls, decorating the entrances to the clubs, all of this so that you go in and see, try, feel, touch. I don't want this kind of sex, if I were alone here I'd turn around and walk away, but I think they're genuinely excited to be here, enthusiastically looking at the signs on the windows as though they're searching for something interesting for them to taste.

"This is the sex shops district," the photographer lets go of The Beauty, turning to me and explaining as if I were a tourist and couldn't see for myself. "I really am a tourist," I remind myself, but I can still see just fine.

He turns to The Beauty, tells her something I can't understand and they share a laugh. Then he places his hands on her waist, she hugs him and they start walking along the street as they embrace, her head resting on his shoulder, and I follow behind.

We pass display windows showcasing mannequins that are dressed in red and black outfits made of fishnet and lace, more and more shops, more and more outfits and stockings and shoes and accessories. They talk among themselves, point and giggle, as if debating what they should purchase and I feel like they're ignoring me, feel like I don't belong. "Are they planning on choosing something for my photoshoot?" I wonder to myself, if so then why aren't they asking for my opinion? I can't understand what they're talking about and I can only guess through their smiles and the tone of their voices as they point at one outfit or another, it's embarrassing me.

"Private show?" a woman from one of the entrances whispers to us. She's wearing a gold-colored mini dress and is standing by a little counter, as if she were a hostess at a Chinese restaurant. Behind her is a golden hallway leading to a closed black door, a worn-out red carpet and photos of bare-chested seductive women hanging on the walls, promising their bodies to anyone who pays up and walks through the black door. "No, absolutely not," I think to myself, but The Beauty and the photographer relish at her offer and start talking to her, it seems like they're arguing over the price and terms of entrance. "Are you sure you're willing to go into this sort of place with them?" I ask myself, why aren't they asking me what I want? What will I do if they go in? Go to the hotel? Part company with them? "Maybe they actually want to go in by themselves and leave me alone here for a few minutes? Maybe she wants to give him a private show? I'll die if that happens." They laugh with the hostess and then say goodbye to her, continue on their merry way as if they've just shared a good joke, I continue behind them and feel less and less like I belong.

"What do you think? Is the outfit nice?" The Beauty turns

and asks me as she points at an outfit with leather straps that's stretched over a mannequin in a shop window, as if she's only just now noticed my existence.

"Yes, very nice," I answer her and smile, happy with the attention, certain that we'll go into the shop to try on the outfit. But she just smiles at me and the two of them walk ahead embraced to the next shop window. I feel insulted by her, I think she only wants to concentrate on herself, throwing crumbs of attention at me. "Then why did you even invite me to join you?" I think to myself furiously, if I wanted crumbs of attention I could get them at the hotel, on a comfy bed in front of a boring TV show.

"Come here," the photographer calls me over while hugging The Beauty, they're standing at an entrance to one of the shops. The large shop window is packed full of mannequins dressed in black lace outfits and chains. I march after them like a loyal and kind-hearted puppy, a puppy that doesn't want to return alone to the hotel right now, and that wants to be petted. "I'm so lame sometimes," I whisper to myself.

After walking in I stay standing in one spot for a moment, taking in the size of the shop. I expected a little shop, a dark little room with a curtain and a salesman with a malicious smile, but this place is huge, hangers upon hangers of clothing and accessories for sex in every size and style imaginable, dimly lit in order to create a bedroom ambience for the clientele. "What kind of people shop here anyway?" I ask myself as I remain in the same spot, looking at the people wandering around the shop. It seems like The Beauty is feeling very comfortable here, thus answering my question. She marches right in and starts checking out the clothing on the hangers with amusement, without any of the embarrassment that I would have felt were I in her place. The photographer walks beside her and looks, his hand placed on her behind as though he's allowing her to have a bit of fun and be playful before he leads her to an outfit or a collar that will satisfy him. Occasionally she slips an outfit off of a hanger, a tiny bra with little to no fabric or a netted top or a lacey overall, presents the item to him with a wide-eyed look so that he can inspect it, and he nods his head for yea or nay, deciding for her if it's right or not.

I stand in embarrassment by the entrance and look as they walk further away from me along the shelves and rails, wondering if to walk in or retreat through the door back to the red neon street. "Try to fit in," I whisper to myself and attempt to emanate confidence, I walk over to one of the rows and start looking through the hanging sex clothes. My fingers slide over black lace dresses, I feel the soft fabric and imagine how it would feel on my body. There are a few dresses that I'm interested in and would like to try on, but there's no man walking next to me from whom I can ask for an opinion and I don't feel comfortable asking the photographer, he's concentrating on The Beauty and I feel like I'd just be bothering him, I try to catch The Beauty's attention to ask for her opinion, but she's far-away already and I don't want to raise my voice. "I need a man," I whisper to myself, "or a good girlfriend that'll pay attention to me." I give up on the excitement of the dresses, despite there being some nice ones, and move on to corsets.

When we came out of the metro station I thought they were

preparing a surprise for me, a sexy outfit for a photoshoot, something especially for me that would make me blush, but now I'm not getting any attention from them. "You, my darling, are living in a delusion of a non-existent photoshoot," I tell myself as I examine the corsets, "you're also not really busy listening to what you were told," I explain the situation to myself, reminding myself that they told me they wanted to find something for themselves, not just for me. And still, they wanted me to join them, so why have they neglected me like this? I feel as though I was invited to a party and no one wants to dance with me, and I stay standing in the corner and look at everyone else dancing and having fun. When we finish with this shop I'll leave, go back to the hotel, one should always know when to quit. The lump of discomfort which has been gone for the past couple of days is slowly returning, collecting in my throat.

I follow them around sedately, I've stopped noticing the clothes, I no longer want to be here, I've had enough of this shop and this street. For a moment they disappear and I rush after them, scared of losing them and staying here on my own, I see them going down a spiral staircase. "Where exactly are we going?" I ask myself as I follow them down, surprised by the discovery of the shop's basement floor. "Does this shop ever end?" I wonder as my astonished eyes are faced with a multitude of shiny leather and latex outfits.

"There's no way I'm trying these on," I explain to myself, remaining on the edge of the stairs, deliberating whether to walk into the basement or to remain in my safe spot. I don't even want to think about how Adam would react were he to see me in this sort of outfit, last time that happened he tossed me aside. "Don't worry, he won't see you, he's gone, remember?" I remind myself of reality. "These two right here aren't that interested in you either," I confront the even more painful reality.

The Beauty is wandering around excitedly among the hanging leather outfits of the basement, and after a while she grabs a dress off the rail and shows it smilingly to the photographer, he approves of her choice with a nod of his head and she gets closer to him, whispers something in his ear and turns to the basement's changing room. "What am I doing here?" I ask myself and feel more and more unnecessary as the moments go by, unnecessary and embarrassed. I survey the basement floor looking for other shoppers who might be as embarrassed as I am but I see no one, we're the only ones here.

"What do you think?" The Beauty asks the photographer, at least I think that's what she's asking him as she slides the changing room curtain aside and smiles in satisfaction. She's wearing a shiny black dress that's revealing her breasts, only covering her stomach and thighs. She stands motionless, blasé to the fact that people can see her white breasts, people like the salesperson who will be coming downstairs any minute now, or maybe a stranger who will soon discover this basement floor, or just a tourist that she happened to find on a street bench.

I can't look away. She has soft breasts, they're not big, they're not perfect and her nipples are small, not like mine. The photographer looks at her and smiles, it's clear to me that he likes what he sees. The Beauty places her hands on her waist, sticks out her chest and slowly shakes her breasts from side to side tauntingly as she smiles at him and completely ignores me. Maybe she likes knowing that I'm looking? Maybe they brought me here so that I can be an onlooker for their games? Add a little spice?

They stare at each other and the photographer slowly steps over to the changing room, gets closer to her, grabs her chin and kisses her hard as he presses her tightly to him. She lays her hands on his neck and caresses him with her fingers. He lets his lips wander down her chin and her neck, grabs her breasts and kisses them roughly, puts her nipple in his mouth and kisses it with force. The Beauty leans back and continues stroking his neck as she tilts her head back and closes her eyes. She slowly opens them ever so narrowly, turns to look at me, as if she's only just noticed me, gives me a little smile and pulls the changing room curtain shut, hiding them from my stare.

And me? I stand motionless and stare, my fingers moving across the fabric of a shiny dress I'm holding, positioned in front of the curtain that's hiding them and trying to stop the lump in my throat. I'm so unnecessary and unwanted, her giggles and breaths hurt me, I think she's trying to stop him, trying to explain to him with make-believe anger that he's exaggerating. I'm not sure, I think that's what she's doing, but I don't want to hear them right now. I want to have someone who'll hug me and kiss me on a romantic vacation and make me feel wanted and like I belong, I don't want to just stand here talking to myself like an idiot. Maybe I should call Adam?

"What's up Adam? I just wanted to tell you that I'm currently in the basement floor of a sex shop and there's a couple fucking or something along those lines behind a curtain, yes, I'm having a great time, a wonderful vacation, thanks for asking." Or maybe I should strike up a conversation with the dresses surrounding me, they'll surely listen and act like true friends. "They're definitely enjoying themselves right now," I explain to the shiny dress I'm holding, "they're having fun and they're not to be disturbed, I'll go ahead and put you somewhere quiet," and I return it to the hanger, trying not to make any noise. "I wonder what they're doing," I turn to a strappy leather dress that would look fabulous on me, "do you think this is their hobby? Picking up lonely tourists like myself and taking them to sex shops so that they can have an audience?" Why did they leave me alone here like this? Why is no one kissing my breasts in a changing room?

Maybe I should actually just go? Quietly retreat? They won't notice if I leave, I should just walk away quietly and disappear on them. Go out to the nasty street? Go into the crowded metro? Why don't you browse through the clothes for a bit longer, they'll probably finish up soon, you're so naïve for thinking you were going to purchase a sexy outfit for your photoshoot. Just look for something nice to think about and stop those tears in the corners of your eyes already.

Sex Shop, a Little While Later
Kate

"Did you see anything you like?" The Beauty turns to me and hugs me from behind, and I kind of ignore her, trying not to look her in the eyes so that she can't see that I had cried, that I got offended.

"No, nothing," I answer her while keeping my eyes on the dresses hanging in front of me, my fingers casually gliding over them.

"Then what will you wear for the shoot?" she asks and I don't turn to face her, I'm looking for an elegant way to wipe my eyes without her noticing.

"What do you think about this corset?" she pulls out a shiny black vinyl corset and hands it to me, ignoring the saleswoman who has just walked down into the basement.

"It looks nice," I give a little smile through my red eyes, take the corset from her and quickly walk over to the changing rooms, making sure to use a different booth than the one she did. On the way there I lower my head as I pass the photographer who's busy tucking his shirt into his pants.

Start by wiping your face, everything will fall into place once you've wiped your face, you're so lame, you're so easily bought. Hang the blouse carefully on the hanger so that it doesn't get wrinkled, hang the knitted top over it, and the skirt on another hanger. Do you really think you'll fit into this corset? Start with the back straps, as though you were putting on a vest, now you just need to get your tummy in and zip it up, stop breathing and slowly zip it up. It doesn't look good with your bra on, take it off, hang it under the skirt, so that it doesn't fall. Be careful not to catch your breasts on the zipper as you pull it up, then you'll really start howling. How does one breathe with this shiny black thing on?

I pull the changing room curtain to the side a little bit, peek into the basement floor, wondering whether or not to step out of the booth. I don't know if they're out there waiting to see me in this incredibly exposing corset, or if I'm meant to decide by myself whether it suits me or not. The Beauty comes over asking if she can come in and I nod to her. She walks around me, passing her hands along my tightly held waist and she seems pleased with what she sees. "No wonder you're pleased now," I think to myself cynically, you got pleasured and I remained a hungry and neglected street cat.

The Beauty pays no attention to my thoughts and pulls me out of the booth, turns me to face the photographer and starts lacing up the corset tightly. I feel my stomach becoming flatter and my breasts pumping up more and more in the tightened corset, it's getting really difficult to breathe.

"What do you think?" She takes me over to the change room mirror and lets me look, it's hard for me to take in how sexual I look in the shiny black corset, I'm not used to thinking about myself in those terms. I look amazing, even I have to admit that to myself. But all I can think about right now is the plain underwear I have on, pink cotton panties with blue butterflies printed on. I want to drop dead, I'm so embarrassed. "How did I not know that I'd end up at a sex shop today, standing almost naked in front of a mirror and wearing a corset? Couldn't I have worn my lacey black underwear?"

I look to the photographer questioningly and he's standing on the side, unashamedly checking me out as if he were meant to be pricing a new toy he's about to purchase for his collection. I caress his name on my arm without noticing and I feel very exposed and embarrassed, regretting that I don't have the lacey black underwear in my bag to change into.

After a few seconds he smiles at me with approval and asks The Beauty, "What do you think?"

"She's beautiful and sexy," she says smilingly, continuously looking into my eyes, as if trying to figure out if I had cried earlier.

I like her answer and I smile at them.

"Shall we look for something additional for the shoot?" he asks and I start getting excited again.

The Beauty walks over to the clothes rail and starts looking for another outfit and I join her in the search, walking around the shop freely, dressed in a shiny black corset which I can't breathe in and is making my breasts look like round balls, completely ignoring the other couple who just arrived in the basement in search for an outfit to suit their sex games.

Later on, when we leave the shop, me with two bags and a smile and the photographer with The Beauty's purchases, she lets go of his hand for a moment, presses against me and brings her lips close to my ear.

"Were you crying earlier?" she asks.

"No, I had something in my eye," I lie to her.

"I'm sorry," she whispers to me.

I smile at her, hoping they'll take me with them so that I don't have to go back to the hotel.

Hotel, Room 314, Early Evening
Adam

"She was here and went back out again," I think to myself as I turn on the lights and survey the room while standing by the front door. She's not here, but her side of the bed is messy, it seems that The Little One had been here and slept. The curtains by the window are drawn open and evening light fills the room. I put my jacket on the bed and sit beside it. Hours of searching throughout the city have brought no results except for the discovery that she had been here while I was out, been and gone. I'm starting to feel like I'm missing something here, I feel like I'm not searching for her in the right places.

"At least she hasn't packed her stuff and gone to a different hotel."

"Plus you bought her a book for a present, that's important." I take the book out of the jacket pocket and look at it. What difference does having this book make if I can't find her?

"I should have waited for her at the hotel," I think to myself with frustration, I wasted hours looking for her all over town and she had been here all along. I get up and wander around the little room, looking for something to do. I spontaneously take my smartphone out and send her a message.

She doesn't reply, I wait and wait and she doesn't reply, I wander around the room for a little bit longer. No reply from her.

Another wander around and a few more minutes pass by and another glance at the silent smartphone.

"That's it, she's decided to screen me."

"Maybe she was busy doing something and didn't hear the message ping?" I try to calm down the feeling of unease.

"Yeah, just like when she didn't hear the message pings when she left me that time, didn't hear the phone for days, whole days without replying to me, until one day she decided to come back," I talk to myself cynically.

"Calm down, she hasn't left you, her things are still here," but no matter how I try to calm myself down it's unsuccessful, I know I'm probably over-exaggerating with my reaction and she'll probably reply soon, but my thoughts are all over the place. I walk back and forth across the tiny room, it's too small and it can't contain me right now.

"Go shower, wash off this day, it'll do you good." I toss the clothes messily on the bed and go to the shower, wash myself off with cool water, so that I get a little bit cold. I want to make myself suffer a bit, take revenge on myself for everything I had done, I deserve a little bit of suffering.

I dry myself with rough strokes, trying to remain collected, but I'm finding it difficult to stay calm. I don't want to stay in the room, sit around and wait for her for hours until she decides to come back here or reply to my message. Waiting for her reply is stressing me out.

Pants, shirt, sweater, everything quickly covering me. The jacket that was laying on the bed and the key card in my pocket, I shut the door behind me and walk through the hallway.

I just feel like I have to get out of that room, get out of this hotel and go, though I'm not sure where to.

Alexandre III Bridge, Evening
Kate

I'm not yet sure where we're going, am I going over to their house with them to do the photoshoot? It seemed so earlier, but now I'm not really sure and I'm finding it uncomfortable to raise the subject. If they don't offer me that soon then I'll part company from them and return to the hotel, I don't want to be a burden, I hate feeling like someone's taking me in out of pity. The photographer is walking behind us, busy with his smartphone, The Beauty and I are walking side by side ahead of him. Little droplets of rain fall occasionally, not the kind that would force us to run through the streets or feel sorry for not having taken an umbrella with us. The boulevard of street lamps across the bridge is fully lit, and the lights of the cars flash against the marble pillars, coloring them yellow.

The bridge is almost entirely barren of people and I don't stall to look at the pretty lights, also ignoring the sparkling Eiffel Tower, which shines from afar as though it were a lighthouse warning me about danger. There's only one couple here, standing with their backs to us, she's leaning on the rail and looking at the water, not at the man standing next to her, he's talking to her and giving her flowers. "I love getting flowers," The Beauty whispers to me and tightens her grip on my arm momentarily. "Me too," I answer her and smile, but I don't stop to look at them, I look at the lights of the cars crossing the bridge.

Taxi ride, Evening
Kate

We're in the darkness of the taxi's back seat, driving through the city. I'm sitting between them, listening to the tires knocking against the wet pavestones of the road. The Beauty's hand is gently placed on my thigh, she's playing with her nails, drawing invisible circles and lines, and the photographer's hand is placed on my other thigh with a sense of ownership, as if I belong to him.

"We've been invited to meet at the club," the photographer announced a few moments prior as we were walking through the streets, leaving me confused, what was I thinking? To be honest, I wasn't really thinking, I was hoping that we were going to his apartment for a photoshoot, but actually I wasn't really prepared for the occasion. I hadn't showered since noon and I hadn't shaved my legs and we never even talked about it. "Do you really want him to photograph you? And what if he'll want more than to just take photos? Do you really want that? You have, I mean, you had a partner for this romantic vacation, do you remember that?" I stood in the middle of the street, looking at the two of them exchanging words which I couldn't understand. Occasionally they added a word or two I could understand but I was already dizzy from all of my thoughts, I needed to stop for a minute and collect myself. I felt like the last few days had been an emotional rollercoaster, I was sometimes happy and laughing and sometimes wanting to vomit.

"Tomorrow night is my last night on this vacation," I said

with hesitation and they paused their discussion and stared at me.

"Excellent," the photographer said after a few seconds, taking on the role of the decision maker, "then come with us to the club."

"And what about my photoshoot, which I haven't yet decided if I really want or not?" I thought to myself sadly, I didn't dare ask. I thought you wanted to photograph me, even though I hadn't shaved my legs and I'm not a model and I'm not that pretty.

The Beauty looked at me and said a few sentences to the photographer, I looked at them, trying to decipher what they were saying, waiting for their verdict.

"Of course," he answered her and looked at me, "and tomorrow night you'll come over and we'll photograph you."

I smiled at him through the darkness. I was on a roller-coaster of thoughts and fears, but I smiled nonetheless.

"Tomorrow is your final night, we'll have to celebrate," he added and smiled back at me.

I wanted to celebrate too, even though I wasn't quite sure how to, and why everything had gotten so messy. I was missing a hug. "I hope you find me a little bit special, and that you haven't simply added me to the list of tourists you collect on a weekly basis like you do your models," I kept my fears to myself, didn't dare say them out loud.

We're in the darkness of the taxi's back seat on our way to the club, or dance bar or something along those lines, and I feel their hands on my thighs. All my senses are sharpened towards the points of contact where their fingers are stroking me, I'm entirely concentrated on the feeling of their fingers over my skin.

The Beauty gently moves her fingers over my thigh, drawing paths along it with the tips of her nails, occasionally scratching me a bit harder, creating a line of moderate pain which she makes sure to quickly stop and caress, while the photographer's hand is holding my other thigh tightly and further up, holding a spot where my skin is more sensitive because of my half-open legs.

"Do you think he'll take his hand further up your thigh the way he did to The Beauty at the party?" Would I stop him? I feel special now, surrounded and enveloped by the attention I was lacking so badly recently. They remain silent, I don't know what to say or think, what do they want with me? Obviously I'm not going to be here in a couple of days, do they talk about me amongst themselves? I could ask The Beauty if we got a moment alone but I'm scared to, the cold outside the taxi scares me too.

The Bridge, Evening
Adam

The cold is bothering me, despite the jacket I took as I left the hotel room, I'm still cold, and I'm pulling it against my body tightly while hastening my steps.

I'm walking through the streets without an actual destination, I cross the bridge. Occasionally I stop to check my smartphone, no reply from The Little One, she's choosing to ignore me. It's difficult for me to think of a clear objective right now, I just feel like I can't go back to the hotel, I have to walk, wander around, do something.

There are hardly any people on the bridge and the only sounds are those of the cars crossing it, the wind must have scared everyone away back to their homes. I stop for a moment to look at the black water and then I notice a bundle of flowers thrown on the sidewalk. "Someone must have dropped them without noticing," I think as I lean over and pick them up, cram them into my jacket pocket.

"Before I give her the book I'll insert petals between the pages, red petals, she'll love that," I think to myself, I hope she'll love it. I feel like a travel agent searching for his long-lost love, with pockets full of flowers and a book and fantasies and hope.

The wind is cold despite my tightly-held jacket but I'm not going back to the hotel. I keep walking through the streets, continuing persistently, stopping for a moment to look at a few young women in short dresses who are trying to get a taxi, probably on their way to a party or a club.

Club, Evening
Kate

"Why did you want me to get revealing clothing for the photoshoot?" I ask the photographer, trying to speak over the loud music. It's hard to hold a conversation with people dancing and music blazing and lights flashing in the background, but I'm intrigued so I decide to ask. We're sitting on a round couch at the side of the club, there's a main dance floor here with people dancing and there are seating areas around it where lights of various colors occasionally flash. The Beauty is sitting between me and the photographer and I'm forced to lean over her in order to get close enough to talk to him, otherwise I won't be heard over the loud music.

The Beauty offers me to swap seats and we do, she leans over me to listen to the conversation, her arm placed on my knee, I no longer have to shout, and I can hear him too. The club is packed full of people and there's an excited assembly of youngsters and alcohol by the bar.

"There's something special about shooting you in an environment that you're not used to," he answers my question.

"I don't understand."

"I'm not interested in your everyday emotions, I want to make you feel uncomfortable, take you to unfamiliar places, that's what interests me," he gives me an examining look, as if evaluating my reaction.

"So I take you to a sex shop and make you try on clothes you hadn't tried on before, and suddenly you start feeling new sensations, shame, breaking inhibitions, daring, shutting yourself off, all sorts of feelings. Some are nice and some aren't, but they all belong to you," he explains and I hope I'm understanding everything he means, this conversation is becoming increasingly interesting and complex. He definitely creates sensations within me, but I'm not going to tell him that.

"After that you return home."

"Return to the hotel," I correct him and he smiles.

"After that you return to the hotel, taking with you the bags of outfits you'd purchased," he's talking and I touch the bags which are placed by my feet, making sure they're near me at all times.

"And you think about the outfits folded inside the bags and you start fantasizing, what's your photoshoot going to be like and which poses I'll be putting you in and what I'll be asking you to do, what you'll agree to do and what you'll refuse." I've been thinking about that since yesterday, I'm just too ashamed to admit it, even to myself.

"And you arrive at my place, ready, with all your feelings and fears." Oh I have a lot of fears.

"And you go to a side room, prepare, or maybe you arrive with your outfit on already." I'll arrive after having prepared in advance, I need to take my time, I need time to think about this exciting and scary thing.

"And you stand in front of me, in front of the camera, and now you're truly exposed." I already feel exposed in front of you.

"And then you meet my desires." I'm sure you have desires.

"And out of that combination a photo is born, that's the photo I'm after, the visibility of your fears, embarrassment, fantasies, everything you feel. Your eyes and your movements will create the life and substance for the photo," he's talking and using his hands to describe his words and I'm listening intently, I get how he charms all the models who want to be photographed by him.

"And doesn't it ever happen that a photoshoot doesn't

work? That the photos don't come out good? That the model changes her mind?" I'm genuinely intrigued, I'm also looking for future escape routes.

"Of course, that happens sometimes." I'm not the only one, just so that it's clear to me, I shouldn't be delusional. I want to ask him about other women he photographed and what The Beauty thought of them and did he sleep with them during the photoshoots too, but I don't have the guts to ask and I don't think he's planning on telling me.

I have loads of questions to ask him, but his smartphone beeps and he asks me to excuse him and turns to answer it.

"Pardon me," he tells me and The Beauty, who's been leaning on me and listening to our conversation. "The people who invited us have just arrived, I'll be right back," and he gets up and disappears into the crowd, leaving me and The Beauty to sit and continue staring at the people around. A few moments later he returns escorted by two women who are obviously famous models and he introduces us, inviting them to join us on the couch.

They're both holding glasses of drinks, smiling at us and looking like they've just walked out of a photoshoot set for a fashion magazine. One's wearing tiny shorts and boots, with endless legs and a smile that belongs to someone who knows her own worth, and the other's in a short silver dress, nonchalantly shaking our hands as if we were merely an obstacle for her to shoo away on her way to the photographer. "I don't think you'll have a hard time shooing away an obstacle such as myself," I think as I look at them with envy, "you're out of my league," and I get closer to The Beauty to make room for them, pushing the bags with my feet to a safe spot near me. "Please don't ask what's in the bags," I think fearfully, "then I'll really be humiliated what with all my photoshoot fantasies, the midget that I am." But I think The Beauty and I are of no interest to them, they're only interested in the photographer. The Beauty didn't even get up to shake their hands, she just gave them a polite smile and she's still leaning her arm on my knee right now, her fingers holding me tighter than before.

The photographer has finished paying attention to me and his body is now turned to the new purchases sitting on his other side, leaving me and The Beauty sitting next to each other, staring at his back and at the people dancing around us.

"Do you want to dance?" The Beauty suddenly asks me.

I'd happily dance with her but I already feel tired from this whole day and from my emotional roller-coaster, one moment I'm getting attention and the next moment I'm being ignored. I'm also worried that if I were to dance with her there would be no one to look after my shopping bags, the photographer definitely won't keep an eye on them, he's wholly busy with chatting to the sparkly women sitting at his side.

"I'm sorry, I'm already tired and these shoes are killing my feet," I answer her and I think the look of disappointment in her face is genuine.

"I need to go to sleep at the hotel, I'm tired," I continue and place my hand on hers, she straightens up and releases her hand.

I pick up my shopping bags and get up to leave, The Beauty gets up and hugs me tightly, I think she would have loved me to take her away from here.

"Call me tomorrow morning, we'll go get you new shoes," she whispers in my ear.

"Thank you for a wonderful day," I whisper back to her.

"See you tomorrow night," the photographer says as he gets up to give me a goodbye hug, "I'll be waiting for you."

The shiny models politely smile at me and quickly return to focus on the photographer.

As I get swallowed amongst all the people on my way out, I stop for a moment, turn around and give them one last look. Partially lit by the club's flashing lights, I see the photographer holding a pen in his hand, grabbing one of the models' hands in his other, smiling at her and starting to write.

Hotel Bar, Night
Adam

"May I ask what you're reading?" the woman sitting next to me at the bar asks me, she's politely sitting two chairs away from me. I don't really understand what she's asking but I think that's what she means.

I don't exactly know where I am and what the time is, and actually I don't care. Earlier I was walking through the streets, watching the cars passing by with an uninterested look, searching for a bar to drink in, and I came across a bar at a fancy hotel. I found myself sitting on a row of barstools, ordering a glass of drink, disconnecting from the people around me, and reading the book which I took out of my jacket pocket. I could hear quiet blues music and whispers of conversations in the background, the bartender was busy polishing glasses and organizing them on the brown shelves behind him, brown shelves filled with expensive whiskey bottles as well as black-and-white photos of the hotel from years ago.

"May I ask what you're reading?" she asks me and interrupts my train of thought. I pause my reading and look at her, she looks to be around my age, wearing a tailored skirt and a buttoned blouse. "She's probably a businesswoman who has just finished her workday and is winding down with a drink," I think to myself. I tell her I only speak English and she repeats the question.

"It's a book of poems, I'm reading poetry," I raise my hand from the page and show her the short lines of text.

"Is it beautiful?" she shows interest, I guess she's a bit bored and is looking for someone to talk to about something, anything, even poetry.

"I think so," I answer, "I only just started reading it."

"May I?" she politely asks and means to ask if she can come closer and sit beside me.

"Sure," I gesture her invitingly with my hand and she comes closer, bringing her glass of drink along. She's sitting close to me and I can smell the gentle scent of her perfume.

We introduce ourselves to each other. I make up a name for myself, a name from a book I read once and liked, I wonder if the name she's just used is real or not and if it even matters.

She asks for the book with her eyes and I hand it over to her, touching her well-groomed fingers for a moment. She looks at the cover, sees the photo and searches for the author's name, and as she opens the book a few petals fall from between the pages and disperse over the bar counter by her glass of drink. She gives me a questioning smile regarding the red petals, I smile back and remain silent, I don't explain about the petals and she doesn't ask, maybe she's shy or just polite. She returns to look at the book and browses through the pages for a few minutes, silently reading the poems before handing it back to me. I listen to the quiet blues music and I look at her as she reads. I look at the soft sepia lights coloring her legs, I focus on how immaculately dressed she is, and on her light-colored lips silently reading the words.

"Read out a poem for me," she asks.

I browse the book for a moment, choose a poem, take a little sip of my drink, place the glass back on the counter and read out a poem to her slowly and quietly. She closes her eyes and gives a little smile, listening to the poem and to the music playing in the background.

"Thank you," she says when I finish. "What do you do for a living, when you're not reading poetry to strangers at hotel bars?" she asks with a smile.

"I'm a simple businessman," I don't tell her the truth, "travelling and moving from one place to another."

"I'm staying at this hotel tonight," she gives me an inviting smile, "would you like to join me in my room, read out more poems to me?"

I place my chin on my hand and look at her for a moment. I know I need to answer her quickly and I don't have a lot of time, I also know that up till now this has been a conversation between a bored man and a bored woman at a fancy hotel bar, and now it's becoming a different type of conversation. I know The Little One has left me, I know she's spending her nights in places unknown to me and I know she's not replying to me, I also know what to decide.

"Thank you for your offer," I smile to the pretty woman in embarrassment, "but you see, I'm looking for a specific special lady to give this book to as a present, and if I keep reading out poems to you she'll never get it, I'm sorry."

She gets up from the chair with a charming smile, and I hope she understood what I said.

"I hope that you find her," she puts her beautiful hand on mine, the one resting on the counter holding the book. "Let me invite you this evening, as a thank you for the beautiful poem," and she takes out a card from her black purse and places it on the bar by our drink glasses.

Hotel, Room 314, Night
Kate

I place the key card on the little table and the shopping bags by the closet and I sit on the bed, take my shoes off, lie back and look up at the ceiling. A simple ceiling, smooth light-colored cream, a few bulbs lighting up the room, I let my eyes wander across it without thinking about anything, let the thoughts calm down a bit after the incredibly turbulent day I had. "I should keep a journal so that I don't forget anything," I laugh to myself as I get up to sit.

"The Tall One," I suddenly tense up, "he's not here." The

room is clean and tidy, the blanket is taut and no Tall One around despite the late hour. Seven quick steps over to the closet and I learn that his trolley is still here, as are his toothbrush and razor in the bathroom.

What happened to him? Where is he now? Maybe something happened to him? Maybe something like, for example, he decided to go sit at a bar somewhere and meet someone else? Or maybe give her a book by mistake? Or maybe he's lying drunk in a ditch somewhere feeling sorry about not wanting me? He definitely has a lot of options, so many options in fact that he's not bothered looking for me for two whole days.

I go over to my bag and take out my smartphone, to my surprise I see a message from him. "Good evening." But the message is from a while ago, I must have been at the club and didn't hear it because of the loud music, the knowledge that he looked for me stirs something inside me. "There you go, he's alive, he wants to tell you he's sorry." Really? Is that what he wants to tell me? Is that why he went to the trouble of writing such a moving message? Don't be such a cynic, maybe he does want to apologize? Then he should apologize, not send me a lame message. Maybe he tried and saw I wasn't replying to him? Then he should try again. Maybe you should call him? There's no way I'm calling him, especially not at this hour, what would I say? He can worry about me for a little bit, let him think I was murdered and that I'm lying dead in a ditch by the river. He didn't want me anymore, so I left, that's life. Where could he be at this sort of hour? Where exactly has he chosen to sleep tonight? Do you think he's planning on telling you?

I hang the new purchases in the closet and look at them with excitement and fear, one is a black leather corset which squeezes my breasts and the other is a shiny black dress which clings to my skin, wrapping and shaping me. I don't believe I'll wear them ever again after tomorrow, but tomorrow is what they're destined for, single-use outfits for one night only, I gently glide my fingers over them, as if I'm trying to determine their worth within my new life.

I slowly undress in front of the mirror, taking off my bra and freeing my breasts after the long day I had, I gently scratch the marks on my skin that the bra had left. I suddenly feel a lack of intimacy. "What if The Tall One walks through the door this very minute?" It suddenly seems weird and inappropriate, as if I'm embarrassed about him seeing me naked. I look at the photographer's autograph on my inner arm, I don't want him to see it, I don't want him to ask questions, I don't want to explain anything to him, I don't want to justify myself. "Maybe I'll lock the door from the inside?" No, you can't do that, that's inappropriate, but I shut the bathroom door as I stand naked in front of the mirror, checking myself out.

The water washes my body and I start soaping myself, careful not to soap my inner arm and the photographer's round autograph, I look at the water streaming over the lettering. I like the round writing but a moment later I remember what happened right before I left the club. I see him turning to the shiny model at his side and starting to write on her arm with a pen, and for a moment I want to scrub off the writing. I deliberate, letting the hot water run over my arm and eventually decide not to erase it, but when I dry myself off, despite the scent of the soap, I feel as though there's still dirt on me, and I make sure not to look at my arm.

"The photographer was right, meeting him and The Beauty has aroused thoughts and emotions within me." I lie in bed with wet hair, feeling clean as well as filthy, looking up at the ceiling again, letting my thoughts wander around before I fall asleep. Squatting in front of him with the corset on, standing in front of him with the shiny dress on, what will he ask me to do? How far will I agree to go? What are my limits? Why did I leave The Beauty at the club with sadness in her eyes? Where is The Tall One?

Day Four

Somewhere in the City, Late at Night or Early in the Morning, Depending on How You Look at It
Adam

A hand is placed on me, touching me and I open my eyes, trying to understand where I am.

I'm not at the hotel by The Little One's side and this is not her hand, this isn't my bed. I had walked through the streets and I sat at a hotel bar, and I drank, there was a woman there and I read her a poem out loud, did that even happen? Maybe I'm just imagining it? Maybe it was a dream?

Yes, it happened, she invited me up to her room to read her more poems out loud.

The hand touches me again.

"Sir, wake up." I think that's what the man who's touching me is saying. He's standing in front of me and handing me my book, explaining with his hands and body language that the book was under the seat and I guess he's asking if it's mine.

Then the woman thanked me and left the bar and I kept wandering around, got on the bus to go back to the hotel and now I'm still on the bus, I must have dozed off. What's the time now?

"Yes, it's mine," I thank him and take the book, I hold it tightly and look at my watch. It's late at night or early in the morning, depending on how you look at it.

The man in front of me continues talking and I don't understand what he's saying, he's gesturing with his hands at the rest of the bus, I look around, the bus is standing and it's vacant of passengers. I think he's gesturing me to get off.

I get up heavily and turn to the door. "Last stop," he tells me and gestures with his hands.

I slowly get off the bus, slowly wake up and I start looking at the street and at the black sky, which is beginning to get morning shades of gray, there are no people on the street, I have no idea where I am.

The man from the bus gets off too and shuts the bus doors, it must be the driver, I think to myself, and I'm stuck here. He walks over to me and talks and explains, pointing to the watch on his wrist.

"Half hour, to the city," he says and I'm guessing he means he'll return to the city in half an hour's time, but it may very well be that I don't understand him at all. He indicates for me to follow him and I do. Just around the corner of the street I discover a simple coffee stand, the kind that never shuts.

"What's in the book?" he asks me as we stand around drinking coffee, at least I think that's what he's asking, since he pointed at the book and asked something.

"This is a book that I want to give to my wife as a present," I explain to him.

"You see, when we had just met, I would give her books, I'd take flower petals which I had found and place them between the pages, so that she would know I love her," I allow myself to tell him the story with the clear knowledge that he doesn't understand me. Even though he's drinking his coffee and listening to me intently.

"And what happened?" he asks, he doesn't actually ask, he just drinks his coffee and looks at me.

"At some point a woman from work asked me to lend her

a book and I did, I didn't remember that it had flower petals between the pages," I slowly tell him and I feel like crying. He'll probably think I'm just drunk.

"And that woman wanted me, because of the flower petals, she thought I loved her and she came on to me."

"That's sad," he says, I mean, I imagine him saying that.

"And my Little One left me because she thought I wanted to cheat on her." The driver gives me an understanding smile, at least he's polite enough to listen to my tear-drenched voice.

"She eventually came back but I was already broken from her having left me, and from then on I just ruined everything," I want to cry on his shoulder but I'm too embarrassed.

"So now I'm with you and I have a book and a cup of coffee and no idea where I am," I finish the story and he looks at me, the coffee stand vendor looks at me too, he's bored and we're the only clients he's got at this sort of time.

"A book, a good woman," he smiles and pats me on the back to cheer me up, pays for my coffee and invites me to return to the bus with him. We walk together, he's walking and talking and I can't understand a word, but I listen to his unfamiliar language and allow myself to wipe away a few tears.

I spend the ride back sitting on the bench by the driver and holding the book tightly. I hope with all my heart that The Little One won't leave me.

Hotel, Breakfast
Kate

"So your husband left you?" the young girl asks me, the one wearing a uniform and standing by a counter at the entrance to the hotel dining room. I tell her the room number and she looks at her lists, notices it's a room for two and looks at me questioningly. "No, he's banished me, he doesn't want me anymore, he told me that very bluntly," I answer her. She doesn't really ask that and I don't really answer her, but she's looking at me silently with a kind of look which makes me certain that's precisely what she's thinking. For a moment she checks to see if he's behind me, assuming he probably got held up on the staircase, and then she realizes no one's coming, at least not anyone who seems like the husband I used to have, so she gives me a little smile and ticks my name off her list.

"If you're that intrigued, I'll have you know that he was actually obtainable this morning," I tell her inaudibly as I walk into the little room, looking for a free table to have my breakfast at. "He was using his smartphone this morning, wherever he was at the time, in this city or in this world." He didn't bother coming back to sleep at the hotel, or calling, but he was obtainable, I wonder where he spent the night? One thing is certain, he didn't spend the night in bed with me.

"Where could he be?" I try to think as I pile two pieces of bread and a slice of cheese on my plate, "Maybe he went to a different hotel?" I wait for the person before me to finish serving himself granola. "That doesn't make sense, he left his trolley in the room," I pour myself a cup of coffee and add milk. "Did he sleep with another woman?" A horrible feeling is creeping up on me and I can't let it go, I have to sit at the table for a moment.

An elderly couple are sitting at the table by the wall, the one with the cabaret dancers' painting and I look at them and at the painting, "They were probably like that too when they were young." I imagine them dancing up a storm and flinging their legs every which way. I look at the man, he's gently slicing his wife's omelet while she's putting sugar in his cup of tea, placing the cup near him so that he can easily reach it, and I start to cry. "It's a shame I didn't believe you back then, it's a shame I left you, even though I came back, it's a shame you banished me."

The smartphone's ping cuts my train of thought as I drink my coffee, and as I quickly turn to my bag the breadcrumbs fall off my dress and my tissue drops to the floor. But it's not him, it's The Beauty asking me what time I'm planning on meeting her, saying she's waiting to go shopping for shoes with me. I reply to her and slowly finish my coffee. The elderly couple in the corner by the painting continue eating their breakfast calmly, his hand gently placed on hers, they speak quietly. The big painting on the wall still has the women dancing, wearing black garter belts and stockings with their legs raised in the air, as the men in suits and top hats look on lustfully. A last glance at the elderly couple and at the painting on the wall, a last sip of coffee and I leave the hotel.

Hotel, Room 314, Morning
Adam

I walk into the hotel room, lock the door behind me, and all I want to do right now is sleep. Sleep for a day or two or a week. I draw the curtains shut, turn the lights off, cover myself with the blanket while lying in fetus position, feeling the fabric on my body, embracing me. I feel safe in the darkness, as if I'm protected from the world. "Just as long as I don't discover anything else that might hurt me," I whisper to the blanket as I think about The Little One. I close my eyes and wait for sleep to arrive. I really want a hug right now.

Streets and Shops
Kate

The Beauty greets me on the street with a warm hug and I smile, I saw her waiting for me from afar, she was looking all around her, searching for my silhouette in the distance, and when she spotted me she gave a genuinely happy smile and marched over towards me until we met with a hug. "Let's go get you some shoes," she crosses her arm with mine and takes charge over our shared walk on a street which is packed full of shops. I like walking arm in arm with her, I feel free and lighter, as though the stay at the hotel this morning brought with it a sense of discomfort which is now slowly leaving me. I want to ask her about how last night ended for them but I feel like that would be impolite, especially if the photographer continued ignoring her and only paid attention to the shiny models. Maybe I should have stayed with her for longer, I squeeze her arm tighter as we continue walking.

What is she even doing with him? Why doesn't she just up and leave him? He's definitely good for a night or two, but to share a life with? I have so many questions for her, but they remain fixed at the tip of my tongue, not venturing beyond. "And that's where they'll stay," I clarify to myself, in the meantime I'm enjoying her company, that's enough, I also have shoes to purchase.

"I can't stand on these things," I think to myself as I try to step on the high heels I'm wearing, this is not what I had in mind when I thought about going shoe shopping with her.

We had been walking along the street and checking out shops when she suddenly stopped in front of a fancy shop which sells party shoes and looked at the window display.

"Let's go in," she told me and I followed her, assuming she wanted to try something on for herself.

"What do you think?" she pointed at a shiny black pair of needle-thin high heels, they had a thick ankle strap made of leather and a big silver buckle.

"Very nice," I answered her.

"They're also really high, I don't think you could actually survive a whole night of walking in them without crying," I thought to myself but didn't say it out loud.

"What size are you?" she asked, I didn't really understand why.

"Size 6," I answered her, that's what it's like for little women, little shoe sizes.

She spoke to the saleswoman and we sat on a leather sofa, waiting for the saleswoman to bring her the shoes, but I started thinking that maybe I didn't totally understand what was happening.

"Who are those shoes for?" I asked The Beauty.

"You," she answered decisively.

"They're beautiful, but they're not my style," I smiled at her.

"And which shoes will you be using for your photoshoot today?" she asked.

I'll admit, I hadn't really thought of that. Last night I thought about how my breasts are going to look at the shoot and how much I'll be willing to reveal them, I thought about the black dress which seemed very sexy and enticing, about whether he'll want to fuck me and about what role The Beauty is playing in this whole scenario. But I hadn't thought about shoes. "You forgot about the shoes," I told myself off. What do the models who go to him for shoots do? I didn't want to think about what the other models do, nor which shoes they have.

I opened the pretty white box that The Beauty passed over to me from the saleswoman's hands, I carefully held the shoe, feeling the thin long heel with my finger, the shoe was beautiful but it was stressing me out, I felt like I was on a train which was taking me on an unclear route and I wasn't entirely sure I'd be able to stop if I so desired. The direction was exciting and intriguing, but I wasn't certain it suited me.

"I'm not sure," I thought to myself silently, looking at The Beauty with a look of uncertainty as I continued to caress the high heel, feeling the narrow edge with the tips of my fingers.

"Do you want us to choose something simpler for you?"

she looked at me with curiosity.

"I don't know." I gave her a deliberating look, I wanted tonight's shoot to be a special experience for me, a one-time occurrence, and I wasn't going to ruin that with inappropriate shoes. I've ruined so many things recently, she couldn't even imagine how many, I didn't want to ruin any more.

"Wait a minute," she told me and turned to the saleswoman, telling her something while pointing at the shoes I was holding. The saleswoman smiled, nodded her head and walked off to the back of the shop.

We waited silently for a moment, I concentrated on the shoe I was holding and she smiled at me and placed her hand on mine, as though she was calming me down.

The saleswoman returned and gave her a white box, she opened it with a smile. "Excellent," The Beauty said. I looked in the box and saw a pair of shoes which were identical to the impossible heels I was holding.

"Let's try them on," she said with a smile, taking her shoes off and arching her foot to fit into the black shoe in her hand.

I smiled at her and tightly arched my foot, shoved it into the shoe and buckled the thick ankle strap.

I'm walking on them very carefully towards the mirror, directing my steps and trying to get used to this height. I feel my chest stretching forward and my breasts sticking out, as if inviting the right set of hands to come and get them. "You're definitely putting out a clear signal here," I tell myself quietly, arranging my dress nicely over my breasts.

The Beauty walks over to the mirror and stands next to me, I think she's used to these types of heels, she's walking with an enviable ease. "She's probably in constant competition with all of his models, she has to be able to walk on such high heels," I think to myself as I look at her beautiful legs. I feel sad for her, for the endless competition she's in.

"What do you think?" she asks me excitedly, checking us out from all angles.

"They're beautiful," I admit to her, "very beautiful." They're not what I thought I'd be purchasing today, but suddenly I envision myself standing in front of the photographer with these crazy shoes on, and I just know I'm going to look wonderful. My imagination is full of thoughts and ideas, and all the fears are currently hiding away in a corner.

I stay standing motionless, looking at us in the mirror, standing close to each other, almost touching. We're wearing autumn dresses with matching shoes and gorgeous legs and I like what I see. We both smile to the mirror.

"If I get these shoes, you're going to have to get them too," I tell The Beauty with a smile.

More Streets and More Shops
Kate

"What do you think? Should we get these too?" I ask The Beauty as I stroll back and forth through the shop and stand in front of the mirror with an examining look, they're pretty and flat and black and comfortable and they suit me. We've been going around different shops, looking for new walking shoes for me.

"They're pretty," she smiles at me approvingly and I smile back. "We'll get them," she tells me without letting me make the final decision and she turns to the saleswoman, pointing and explaining as I get my wallet out to pay. "Do you want to keep them on?" she asks me, and even though I hadn't thought of it before, it seems like a good idea to me, I'm sick and tired of my shoes and the pain they've been inflicting upon me, they were much more comfy back home, but on the paved streets of this city they're really torturous.

The Beauty tells the saleswoman something and I hand her my old shoes so she can throw them away, I silently say goodbye to them, but the saleswoman puts my old shoes in a new box and hands it to me, I'm embarrassed and I don't understand what's happening, I take the box and pay her.

"Why did she give me my old shoes back?" I ask The Beauty as we leave the shop and return to the street.

"Because I told her we want to donate your old shoes," she explains.

"We want to donate them?" I ask with happiness in my heart.

"Of course not," she answers me, "They're old and uncomfortable, they should be thrown away," she smiles at me.

"So what then?" I don't entirely understand her intention.

"I know exactly where we're going to throw them away," she smiles and takes me by the hand.

The Bridge, before Noon
Kate

"You're not really planning on throwing them away here," I tell her with genuine concern, imagining my final vacation day being spent in jail for having thrown items into the river, or even just getting a fine from an angry cop.

"Of course I am," she answers me with a mischievous smile, "This is precisely the right place for getting rid of anything unnecessary," she laughs.

We're standing in the middle of the bridge, leaning on the white marble rails and looking at the greenish water flowing serenely beneath us.

"We shouldn't do it, we'll be seen," I continue with my concerns.

"Who's going to see us?" The Beauty retorts.

I look around, the bridge is packed full of tourists with cameras, pedestrians, and a few couples taking photos of themselves, I'm trying to understand if she's serious and is trying to test my limits or if she's just joking.

"There are hardly any people here," I answer her and laugh, pointing at the crowd surrounding us.

"So what?" she replies and gets closer to me, "they'll think we're special."

"We're special as it is," I laugh back, "even without tossing old shoes into a river."

"Then what should we do with them? We have to get rid of them," she insists and I think to myself that I really like her, I'd love to have a friend like her.

She takes a moment to think and then grabs my hand and we walk across the bridge with light footsteps, passing the tourists and cameras by, we reach the end of the bridge and go down the stairs that lead to the riverbank.

I feel a lot braver under the bridge, there are no people on the riverbank, except for a tourist boat which is sailing in the distance. I can hear the noise of the cars crossing the bridge over us, lightly shaking the metal support beams.

"Come on," The Beauty urges me with excitement and I pull out the old shoes from the box and quickly toss them, rushing so that I don't change my mind, hoping no one can see me, I don't want to be that tourist who ended up spending the night in jail. If I had expected some feeling of relief I'd be disappointed right now, I don't feel anything, it's only The Beauty's clapping and shouts of "Bravo" that make me smile and feel a little bit more like I'm special.

"You did it," she smiles at me as we climb up the stairs back to the bridge, "You got rid of your past." And I smile at her and think to myself that these sentences are nice, but they're actually making me think about The Tall One and why he still hasn't called me and where did he sleep last night.

"I hate them," she suddenly says. We're sitting on the white marble stairs on the side of the bridge, enjoying the autumn sun and I think I know who she's talking about, but I don't ask her.

"It's a shame you left last night," she continues and I stay silent and listen to her.

"I wanted you to stay with me for a little bit longer." I'm sorry I left, even though I was really tired.

"It's a shame that I left."

"We go to those clubs and then they show up, wanting to meet him because he's considered famous and he can advance their careers and I hate it." She takes out a cigarette and offers me one. I turn her down with a smile of gratitude and she lights one up for herself, stays silent for a moment, playing with the smoke.

"They come over to sit with us at parties and events, they join us and they wear tiny miniskirts and no underwear, they sit in front of him with their legs open, showing him what they have to give him in return," she continues and I gently place my hand on her arm.

"They ignore me, as if I don't even exist. And the worst thing is that when he sees them and their open legs, he ignores me too." I notice a tear running down her cheek.

"And I have to remain at the parties with him, I have to dress nicely and smile with perfect teeth and perfect lipstick, look away as he turns his back to me and busies himself with impressing some new young girl with beautiful words about art." More tears start running down The Beauty's cheeks and I feel like I want to cry for her too. I gently take the cigarette from her hand, I take one drag from it, let the smoke blend through my mouth and I give her back the cigarette, placing it between her fingers.

I'm looking for something I can say that would cheer her up and I can't think of anything, I want to tell her that she doesn't have to stay with him, that she can get up and walk away, that she'll be better off without him. But that's condescending, I don't really know her, I don't have the right to advise her on these matters, all I can do is be there for her right now.

"Yesterday, after you left, he didn't pay any attention to me at all," she says while crying and I sit closer to her and hug her.

"He talked to them and then he danced with them and I just sat and smiled, just like that, smiled to myself like an idiot." I hug her tighter and place my head on her shoulder.

"I wish I had stayed," I whisper to her and gently caress her hair.

"We would have smiled at each other," she laughs with tearful eyes and then wipes them.

"He's not a bad person, but he only thinks about himself and his photography and his freedom," she says and I want to scream at her to leave him, but I hug her instead.

"And everyone wants to sleep with him, they do it happily, they see it as part of the fun, part of the experience. Then they continue on to their next adventure and I'm the only one who stays in the same place, unable to make any changes." I feel ashamed for being one of those women.

"And what about me?" I ask her, scared of her answer.

"And I know I need to make changes, but I don't have the strength to do it," she continues, ignoring my question.

"And what about me?" I ask again, feeling even more scared.

She takes a drag from the cigarette, looks at me and smiles, "I like you, I want you to be photographed by him, I want to give you that gift, he's an excellent photographer, it really is quite an experience." I look at her, hoping she means what she says, I think she does.

"Them, I hate," she clarifies.

"Maybe we can be photographed together," I offer her, feeling a little bit more confident.

"Maybe, if it's appropriate," she answers and gives me a little smile, and I'm not sure if she means it or if she has other plans in mind.

"We already have matching shoes," I point to our shopping bags and we look at each other and laugh a bit through the tears.

We sit silently for a while, looking at the passers-by who are crossing the bridge, some of whom stop to look at the water or to take photos, and I gently caress her arm.

"He knows how to listen to me, look into my eyes, look into my very soul, so that I feel like he cares only for me." I listen to her and feel like she's trying to explain to me, or to herself, why she hasn't left him yet.

"And then suddenly he doesn't care about me and he goes with someone else and I break down." I feel her body beginning to cry again.

"When he wrote his name on my arm I felt like the most special woman in the world," she says and my hand, which has been caressing her arm, freezes in its place.

"Of all the gorgeous girls that surrounded him, I was the one that he chose. And I was so proud of us that I went and got it tattooed," she wipes her eyes with her inner arm and the tattoo of his name.

"And then, a while later, I realized that this is his beloved signature, which he signs on all the women he shoots, it's his trademark." She cries again and I hug her, feeling a stinging sensation on my inner arm, where his writing is, as if I have a burn on the place where he had put his name.

"You know, that's his unique stamp, just like he wanted, everyone who follows his photography always looks for the signature, trying to find it on the model's body, her hand, her leg, her throat, neck, breasts, all sorts of places." Now I really want to scrub his trademark off of me, erase it as though it had never even been there.

"And every time I look at photos he's taken of someone else I think to myself, where am I going to discover his signature on her this time?" I want to tell her something comforting and I can't find the words.

"I know you have one," she smiles at me through her tears, "I have one too, and mine can't come off in the shower." I smile back to her with gratitude.

"It's not simple, being a famous photographer's girlfriend," she sums everything up with a smile.

"Don't remove his signature," she tells me as our silence lengthens.

"I feel uncomfortable," I answer her honestly.

"I want you to come over," she insists and puts her arm around me.

"I prefer for him to be with you, someone that I like, than with the others, whom I hate," she says and it's not clear to me if it's the shoot she's referring to. Should I ask her?

I'm trying to think of something that would make her feel good, something that would make me feel good, I want her to know that I don't want to hurt her.

"Then you should sign your name on me too," I say. She looks at me, not quite understanding what I mean.

"So that I'm marked by you as well," I try to word the idea that I'm slowly constructing, "so that you too will have a signature that can be visible during the shoot, not just him, you'll belong there too," I smile at her and give her my other hand.

"You want me to mark you too?" she takes my hand and asks, trying to clarify.

"Yes," I answer her excitedly, "That way, every time you'll look at my photos, you'll search for your signature instead of his, and you'll remember me with a smile, not like all the others," I conclude my idea.

She thinks for a moment about what I've suggested, she seems to like the idea.

"Do you have a pen?" she asks.

I take the pen out of my bag and present it to her, she puts its tip against my hand, which is placed on her lap, thinking about how to write her name, she pauses and then hands me the pen back.

I give her a baffled look.

"I'm not him," she tells me with glistening eyes, "I want to sign my name on you differently."

She goes through the bag which is hanging on her shoulder by a thin strap and takes out a black eyeliner. She holds my hand, gently folds my fingers to make a fist, and starts to daintily draw her name on my knuckles, each finger bearing a black letter, writing her name on my hand like they do with tattoos.

She's concentrated on her work, slowly drawing the letters, and I'm making sure not to move my fingers as I stare at her focused face and her lips, which are inaudibly mouthing her name. I'm moved by her.

"What do you think?" she asks when she finishes, giving me an anxious smile, examining her name written in black bold letters.

I make a fist with my hand and place it under my chin so that the writing is visible, smile at her and say, "It's perfect."

She laughs and wipes the tears from her red eyes.

"I would have loved you to be my friend," she says, "but I know your vacation is coming to an end and that we won't see each other again."

"Let's go walk around for a bit," I get up and give her my hand, and we start walking towards the hotel.

Hotel, Room 314, Noon
Adam

"What are the chances of you beating that?" I ask myself and feel incredibly low. The closet doors are open because I wanted to take out clean clothes from my trolley. My eyes are fixed on a shiny black dress and a leather corset, sticking out in comparison to all of The Little One's other clothes, like a road sign which can't be ignored.

"Why did she get these clothes?" I whisper and I'm finding it difficult to handle this discovery. Does she want to wear them for me? No way considering what I had told her the other morning. "Then who did she get them for?"

I don't know what to think, I feel like the entire world is collapsing on top of me. Her clothes are hanging in the closet and her suitcase is here, but her thoughts and intentions are no longer aimed towards me, they're elsewhere. "It's only a matter of time before she comes to get her things and then completely disappears from my life," I tell myself. I have to drink something.

I walk over to the room's minibar, little bottles of whiskey are sparkling at me promisingly, but I ignore them and go for a sugary orange soda and a chocolate bar. I have to think for a moment, calm myself down.

I look at the open closet doors again. The shiny dress and the corset look like they're giving me a smile of victory and contempt. I walk over and stare at them from up close with a hostile look, "I could throw you away in the trash," I explain to them, determined to beat them.

"Really? Is that what'll stop her from leaving?" I ask myself cynically as I glide my hand over the dress's fabric. "Do you think that if you talk to the clothes or throw them away in the trash then The Little One won't leave?" I feel like I've been defeated.

"Yes, you've been defeated, someone else is going to enjoy my Little One while she wears a shiny dress and a leather corset." You wanted to be mean to her? You wanted to ruin the vacation? You wanted her to leave? Then you got what you wanted, she went off and found herself some thrills, she deserves to have fun. I feel like my thoughts are starting to repeat themselves, screening a disturbing movie in my mind.

"No," I explain to my thoughts, I wanted her to hold me tight and tell me she's sorry and promise me that she'll never leave me again. So, I bought her a book.

"That's what you bought her? A lousy poetry book?" I look at the book, it's placed on the bed looking lame and neglected, I point to the closet with my eyes, "What are the chances of you beating that?" The book looks like it's ashamed of itself.

"Maybe I should leave her before she leaves me?" I think to myself, at least that way I'd be saving a little bit of my dignity, I'll be able to walk away with pride, not just sit around waiting for the knife to come. I'll leave calmly, in a dignified way, I'll just go.

I go over to the bathroom and collect my things, put them in the suitcase. They don't seem to leave a noticeable vacuum behind, I don't think I'll be leaving a lot of sorrow behind in this room, as it is my trolley has hardly been opened during this vacation.

The little bit that there was to pack is already packed, the trolley is placed in waiting at the bottom of the closet and I lie on the bed, look up at the light ceiling, try to collect my thoughts and decide what to do, but the same thought repeats itself in my mind over and over again, "She's going to leave me."

Boulevard Saint-Germain, Noon
Kate

"Why did he leave you?" The Beauty asks me as we walk around the boulevard casually, looking at the brown autumn leaves, and I'm surprised by her question, I feel like I need to sit down for a moment and I look for a bench.

I wonder to myself how much and what I should tell her, and where to even start, I have no idea. "We broke up because of a book," I answer, "Because of a book with flowers."

"Please tell me," she asks and I feel like I can't turn her down after she had opened up to me the way she did, it also seems like her interest is genuine.

We sit down and I look at the warm afternoon sun, its pleasant warmth makes me close my eyes, the pain of my story is also contributing to that.

"I used to have someone, a charming guy, we were together for a few years," I begin the story. I can't bring myself to tell her that we're still married.

"How did you meet?" she asks with the excitement of a close friend who wants to know all of the details.

"At a party, he was tall and handsome with loads of women surrounding him, kind of like your photographer," I smile at her and then think that maybe I made a mistake by mentioning the photographer, but her expression remains the same and I continue. "I saw him from afar, I took a liking to him," I recall the first time I laid eyes on him, "the power of his hands as he spoke, the way he moved them, everyone was transfixed by him, he was describing a nature hike he had been on or some sort of world-travel adventure on some faraway island, he really knew how to express himself with a lot of sensitivity."

The Beauty is listening to me with fascination.

"And as you already know, I'm pretty small, it's a bit difficult for me to stand out in a crowd," I smile and she does too.

"So, I waited for the right moment and then asked him a really interesting question."

"What did you ask?"

"I don't actually remember anymore," I answer her honestly, "it had something to do with books, it wasn't connected to what he had been talking about, but it immediately got his attention. But I hadn't yet fallen in love with him at that point," she's fully attentive and I continue.

"We started going out and we felt really good together, and then one day, as I was reading a book - I like reading books - I discovered some petals between the pages. Someone had put flower petals in there to dry. I found it strange and smiled to myself. A few days later I was reading a different book and discovered that it too had dried petals hidden within its pages." She smiles at me.

"I learned that while we were taking walks together, casually through a field or even in the city by a nice garden, he'd pick flowers and put them in his pocket. When he realized I liked reading books, he started hiding the flower petals between the pages, for me to discover as I read them."

"That's how I fell for him," I smile at the memory of what was, and look at The Beauty who is listening to me with wide open eyes lit by the autumn sun.

I think about Adam, I miss him and I miss his flowers between the pages, and tears start collecting in the corners of my eyes.

"And why did he leave you?" She places her hand on my knee and looks at me softly, and I don't quite know how to tell her what had happened.

"He gave a book with flowers in it to someone else, a book which had been mine, and I couldn't handle that, it really hurt me, she fell for him straight away and they started an affair, so I up and left."

I'd like to tell her it had all been a mistake, but I can't get myself to do it. I'd like to tell her he had innocently lent the woman the book, forgetting it contained the petals he had placed in it especially for me, and that I had been angry with him and wouldn't listen to anything he said. I'd like to tell her that they didn't really have an affair, that the woman had fallen for him and tried to seduce him, and that I refused to believe that nothing had happened between them. I'd like to tell her what had really happened, but then she'd think I'm an idiot and I can't handle that right now, it's enough that I think that about myself. I'm such an idiot and I deserve him not wanting me anymore.

"And you didn't try to forgive him?" The Beauty asks me gently.

"I tried," I say with a sad, teary smile, "I tried to go back to him, but he wasn't prepared to forgive me for having left him," I give her the partial truth.

Now I'm properly crying and The Beauty hugs me and caresses my neck.

"So now I'm here on a romantic vacation with you," I say as I wipe my face and laugh cynically through my tears.

She remains silent, hugs me, caresses my neck and gets me a tissue out of her bag, my tears keep running.

We sit quietly on the bench and look up at the sky and the sun, I try to calm down and she smokes silently. She offers me a cigarette but I politely turn her down, one or two more of those and I'll take up the habit again, I've made enough mistakes recently, I don't want to get carried away and make another one.

"Let's go buy you a book and I'll put flowers in it," she suddenly offers, interrupting my train of thought, I'm moved by her gesture and my tears threaten to return.

"Thank you," I say with a smile and wipe my eyes with the tissue, "your offer is lovely and I really appreciate it, but the book with the flowers belongs solely to him."

We continue to sit silently on the bench, side by side, she's enjoying the sun's warmth and smoking a cigarette, I'm enjoying the sun's warmth and occasionally wiping away my tears, thinking about books and about tonight.

"Let me walk you to your hotel," she gives me her hand and we rise from the bench.

Hotel, Room 314, Noon
Adam

"Don't give up on her," I stare at the light ceiling, waiting for an idea. "Don't surrender to the dress and the corset, it doesn't matter why she got them or who she got them for. You want her? Then fight for her." I whisper encouraging sentences to heighten my motivation. But it's not easy, I feel like all hope is lost, pep talks might work for romantic movies, but do they stand a chance in real life? Do I stand a chance against the outfits awaiting in the closet?

"Try to be yourself. She'll fall in love with you now just like she did back then," I try to convince myself. That sentence is lame, banal and corny, but it's the best I can do right now. Either I do that or I give it all up, and if I decide to give up then I'll need to get my trolley out of the closet and get out of here.

"Fuck you, I'm going to win, I'm not giving up, I've got an idea," I tell the outfits as I get off the bed. For a moment there I catch myself standing in front of a closet shouting at clothes, it seems so ridiculous that I start laughing, smiling to myself in the mirror. Should I go out to the city in order to beat the outfits, or should I shower first?

Hotel, Hallway Leading to Room 314, Noon Kate

I'm in the short hallway connecting between the staircase and the room when I suddenly realize I may have made a terrible mistake. "What if Adam is in the room right now?" I think to myself with horror. But I can't back out now and I pass by the cleaner who is going through the rooms with her service cart. She greets me and I give her a little smile, but I've only got one thing on my mind. "Please let him not be there, please let him not be there." My shaky hand goes through my bag looking for my wallet, I get the key card out and get closer to the door.

The Beauty and I had been walking around the city like a couple of old friends, holding shopping bags, and we stopped for a goodbye hug outside the hotel entrance.

"I need the bathroom," she told me with embarrassment, a moment before we hugged goodbye.

"Come up to my room," I offered her spontaneously without thinking too much about it.

"Thank you," she smiled.

"Now this is real sisterhood," I thought to myself as we entered the hotel lobby.

We were walking through the hallway leading to the room, the wall-to-wall carpet absorbing the sound of our footsteps, when suddenly I remembered Adam and realized he might be in the room.

I stopped for a second, not knowing what to do.

"Is everything alright?" The Beauty asked.

"Yes, yes," I smiled at her, trying to conceal my thoughts, "I thought I had the wrong floor," and we kept walking, I was terribly scared.

"What will you tell her once you open the door and see him there? What will you say? Figure something out already, what will she think of you? What are you going to do?" I felt like I was starring in a thriller where the actress is walking in slow-motion towards a predictable and irreversible end. I slowly walked towards the room, smiled at the cleaner who passed by us, trying to think up an excuse or an explanation or a justification, and I couldn't. The only thought I had in my head was, "What will she think of me after I had lied to her like that?"

I stopped by the door, got the key card out of my wallet and smiled to The Beauty, who was looking at me as if saying, "Open it already, I have to pee."

"Maybe she'll rush to the bathroom and not notice there's a man in the room?" I think to myself, "I could tell her he's my brother, if he isn't naked that is, yes, that could work too." Not really, even I wouldn't believe me.

I open the door to the room, say a silent prayer and walk in, The Beauty follows me.

The room is empty, I look around, waiting to see Adam peeping out of a corner, but he's not here. The room is neat and tidy as though housekeeping had just finished cleaning it, the blanket is stretched over the bed, the curtains are wide open, no Adam in sight. I take a couple of deep breaths of relief.

"May I?" The Beauty asks, cutting my train of thought.

I look at her, not getting what she means. For a moment, while searching for Adam in the room, I had forgotten she was there. She hints towards the half-open bathroom door with her eyes and I finally recall why she's here.

"Of course," I step back to allow a pathway for her in the little room, thinking for another terrifying moment that maybe he's in the bathroom, but it's too late for me to do anything about it. My eyes follow her as she crosses through the room, turns the bathroom light on and shuts the door behind her.

No screams are heard, I assume she hasn't met with him in there. I sit on the bed to rest for a moment, rest and calm down my racing heartbeat.

"She'll probably spot his toothbrush and razor and understand that there's also a man staying here," I now realize the problematic aspect of letting a stranger into my hotel room, but I can no longer handle all this stress and the pounding of my heart. "Let her find out, let her say that I'm a liar, let her get offended and leave." I'm unable to explain myself and I have no excuse to offer her when she asks. I stay seated and scan the room, looking for a sign of him, there's not even a hint of his presence. Maybe he's finally left me.

I hear the toilet flushing behind the closed door and prepare myself for the questions that will bombard me once the door opens.

"Is everything alright?" The Beauty appears through the bathroom door, asking me with a worried look.

"Yes, why do you ask?"

"Because you suddenly seem tired, or sad." Either she hasn't noticed his toiletries or she's too polite to ask, the second option seems to make more sense to me, I feel completely exhausted by all the stress of this scenario.

"No, everything's fine," I smile at her, hoping she believes me.

"Are you worried about tonight?" I feel like she doesn't want to leave and is trying to find things to talk about, I think she wants to stay here and chat with me but I want to wind down a bit, rest a bit, I've also got Adam flooding my mind, he's left me, for good.

I collect myself and stand up, I don't want her to think it's because of her and get offended, and I don't want her to think that I'm scared about tonight or that I don't want to come over, I just want some time to myself. How do I say that without hurting her feelings?

"Not at all," I say with fake cheerfulness, "tonight's photoshoot will be really special and I'm looking forward to it."

I think she's waiting for me to say something additional.

"I had a lovely time with you today, I'll rest for a while and prepare for tonight," I say and hug her, I think that's what she was waiting for.

"I'm so happy I met you, you fill me with courage," she says and hugs me for longer than usual, as though she doesn't want to part company, and I feel like I could tell her the same thing, if I weren't so worried about Adam's toiletries, did she notice them or not?

My eyes follow her as she walks down the hallway. "See you tonight," I tell her.

"Tonight," she replies as she walks away, keeping her back to me and lifting the shopping bag with the shoes up in the air. I watch her walk away from me on the pink wall-to-wall carpet until I lose sight of her.

The second I shut the door I go straight to the bathroom and turn the light on. The glass by the bathroom sink has my toothbrush and razor, Adam's things are gone. Four swift steps to the closet, his trolley is still in there. I sit on the bed and then lie back, looking up at the ceiling, I have to rest and calm down a bit, I need coffee.

The Latin Quarter, Café, Afternoon
Kate

"Are you waiting for someone?"

"No, I'm alone."

I sit at a café, choosing a corner table by the window, already feeling a little bit more like I belong. Two chairs facing each other, other tables scattered around, large windows looking out to the hectic street, a light afternoon breeze enters the café.

I hang my bag on the back of the chair and place the smartphone on the table, facing me, I sit back and stare at it.

Black-and-white checkered floor tiles leading to the outdoors' noise of the street, a few youngsters sitting at the tables outside the café. They're arguing loudly and their voices penetrate the café but I can't understand what the argument's about, a young couple sitting close to me, busy with themselves. I feel like nothing's changed here, the same youngsters who never run out of things to say, the same loved-up couple staring at each other, the same waiter with the same manners.

I look at my blood-red nails. I imbed them into my palm until it turns red, I press them in harder and stronger, momentarily enjoying the sensation of the pain, and I let go. I'll go back to my hotel room soon and redo my nail polish.

"What would the lady like to order?"

"Coffee, espresso please."

The smartphone is black and silent, I lift it up, play with it, turn it and place it back on the table, lift it up again and place it down again.

I feel good relaxing in front of the wide open windows that show the street, looking at the passers-by as they rush, trying to invent life stories for them, at least for the ones who hang back for long enough so that I can catch a proper glance at them.

"There you go," the waiter carefully places the coffee down.

"Thank you," I look at the waiter and then return my gaze to the passers-by outside, letting the silent hustle-bustle calm me down. I'll go back to the hotel to get ready soon, I'll fill myself up with thoughts and adrenaline, but right now I don't want to think about anything. I want to be an anonymous woman, sitting alone at a little café drinking an espresso. Drinking and smiling to herself for the woman that she is.

My silent black smartphone suddenly pings.

"Surprise, The Tall One came back," I smile to myself and to the shift manager who passes by my table and smiles back at me.

"I forgot to give you our address and the entrance code to the building, kisses." It's not him after all, he must be busy with other things.

The Latin Quarter, Another Café, Afternoon
Adam

I think the only reason they haven't thrown me out of this café yet is because I'm a tourist, considering all the paper clippings and the mess I've made around me. That and the fact that I ordered a cup of coffee and the cheesecake that I like makes them feel too uncomfortable to show me out the door.

I place the poetry book in front of me on the table and begin working.

"Red rose petals." I'm scattering them between the pages for you, because I love you and because I want to give you a present, a poetry book. The petals are our exclusive thing. I found the roses on the bridge, I'll tell you all about it one day.

"A purple pencil drawing of a huge suitcase on one of the

pages, carried by a man I couldn't quite manage to sketch properly." Because you like to bring a lot of clothes with you and I love the fact that you want to surprise yourself as well as me each and every morning. I'm sorry I didn't help you with your suitcase.

Thank goodness I found an arts and crafts shop at the end of the street.

"A piece of white ribbon glued over a poem, I found it wrapped around the marble rail on the bridge." Because I know how excited you get about brides in white dresses and because you need to know that I'm moved by our marriage, it's the best thing in my life.

How do you explain to a salesman at an arts and crafts shop that you need glue and scissors if he doesn't understand a word of English? I'll write a play about that one day.

"Your lips, the way they look when I summon them in my mind's eye, I cut them out of a magazine that I bought on the street and glued them on a page." I searched for them through dozens of magazines until I found the right ones, the newspaper vendor was starting to get upset with me.

"A sketch of the bridge drawn over the words of one of the poems, the best bridge I could draw, I'm giving you flowers and you're smiling, though your smile didn't come out that clear." It didn't happen on this vacation, but it's what I would have wanted to happen to us.

"The label of a sexy outfit I purchased for you at a sex shop, to replace the one you wore when I insulted you. Something private just for the two of us which I find amazing, and I'm sorry about having insulted you." Do you know how many sex shops there are on that street?

"A painting I saw at a museum and cut out of an art book, two men sitting with one woman, I allowed myself to erase one of the men with a marker pen, it seemed more appropriate that way, one man and one woman, just like us." I bought the book at a photography and art bookshop that I came across, one day we'll go there together and look through all the photos and paintings.

"A bag of brown sugar that I stole from this café and glued onto a page, in honor of all the cafés that we didn't sit at together during this vacation." We'll have to come back here again and make amends.

"An Eiffel Tower keychain that I bought for one Euro at a shop in the Latin Quarter." An entire Paris vacation without climbing up the Eiffel Tower and without kissing you, I miss you so much.

I close my book-present, now I just need to let the glue dry for a little while, collect all the paper clippings scattered around me, and finish my coffee and cheesecake.

And find The Little One.

Hotel, Room 314, Early Evening
Kate

I've got that feeling at the bottom of my stomach again, but this time it's from excitement. I've put the back of the toilet seat down and I have my foot placed on top of it, my hand slides over my leg with the razor, first downwards with the direction of the hair and then back up. The bathroom is steamy from the shower I just had and I feel pleasantly warm. The sensation of the razor sliding over the hair conditioner I had put on my leg makes me feel sexy. I usually tend to use Adam's shaving foam, if he were to ever find out about that he'd freak out, but he's not here anyways, and his toiletries have vanished along with him, so I make do with hair conditioner.

I use my fingers to stretch my stomach up, the same stomach with which I have a complex relationship, and which today I'm willing to make peace with for the sake of the approaching evening. I make sure to stretch the skin properly and I pass the razor over the little corners which I usually leave to grow wild, being extra careful not to cut myself.

A last rinse of the hair conditioner from my legs, I slide my hand across and examine my smooth skin, I wipe the steam off the mirror, I'm wrapped in a towel and ready for my makeup.

Delicate makeup on my face and eyes, I want to look my best.

Careful with the eyeliner over my lashes, I don't usually color them this way, but today I want to feel fierce.

Dark eyeshadow, I think it'll suit the black dress.

I finish applying the eyeliner and look at my eyes with satisfaction. I place my hand in front of my face, leaving a little gap between the fingers through which I can see myself in the mirror. I see The Beauty's name written on my fingers and I see my eyes peering through them, I like what I see.

I toss the towel aside and stand naked in front of the mirror, checking myself out. Despite the shower, I can still see the bra strap marks on my shoulders from today's walk. I think they might spoil the photoshoot, maybe I should go there without a bra on? I'll leave it here. What about underwear? Will they leave a mark on my hips? Should I go commando? Isn't that a little bit over the top? I don't know what to decide.

I carefully apply the lipstick, I want to stay within the lines, I hate messing it up and then having to fix it.

I wander around the room in the nude for a few minutes, I want to let the lipstick dry before I get dressed. I get a little bit cold and I wrap myself in the towel again, walk over to the window and stare down at the street. I search for interesting people to look at, but the street is nearly empty, everyone's rushing to their homes at this time of the day, no one's taking their time to wait for anyone. Even if some stranger were to look up, all he'd see would be a regular woman wrapped in a white towel, looking out of a hotel window, that's not really something to write home about.

The dress and the corset are laid out on the bed, I still can't decide which one to wear and which one to take in a bag with me.

"Who volunteers to go first?" I ask them, but they exercise their right to remain silent. Eventually I go for the dress, despite how short and revealing it is, it still seems like the more decent of the two, at least for the beginning, and also that way I can get The Beauty to help me with lacing the corset later on.

My breasts almost pop out of the dress and I fix them back in. "Behave yourselves," I tell them off affectionately, "no red nipples today."

I put a long knitted dress on top, so that I don't attract too much attention on the street, and also so that I don't get too cold. The shiny dress's fabric is tight against my skin and the knitted dress is sliding over it.

Put my red suede boots on, push the lipstick into one of them.

I transfer the contents of my bag into a smaller black bag which I had brought for nights out, I find a box of condoms and a box of Band-Aids, some with gel and a few with Donald Duck.

A shopping bag containing the corset, and inside it another bag containing the shiny black high heels.

Bag, silent smartphone, key card, coat, seven steps to the door.

Two deep breaths as my hand grabs the door handle. "I can change my mind at any time," I repeat to myself.

I'm ready.

And still no sign of Adam. It's time to go.

Hotel, Hallway Leading to Room 134, Early Evening
Adam

I come out of the elevator, I'm full of excitement, I walk through the short hallway towards the room. My hand is wrapped around the book, holding it tightly, as though I'm scared it'll drop and disappear forever.

The door to our room opens and I freeze with anticipation, I see The Little one coming out. To begin with she doesn't notice me, her eyes are turned towards the door as she shuts it. Then she turns around and sees me, and she freezes too.

All the beautiful words and sentences I had prepared in my mind have now vanished and I stand there silent for a moment, looking at her, smiling awkwardly. Say something already.

She's also standing and smiling embarrassedly, as if waiting for me to say something. She waits for a second and then starts walking towards me. For a moment I think that maybe she wants to come and hug me, but the direction of her steps clarifies that she wants to pass me by. She really isn't interested in me anymore.

I make room for her to walk past me in the narrow hallway and I touch her hand as she passes. "Little One, I'm sorry, I need to talk to you," I manage to squeeze out the best possible sentence I can think up.

"Tomorrow, we'll talk tomorrow," she quickly answers me, continuing down the hallway to the elevator, leaving me standing and watching her back as she gets further away. She pauses by the elevator for a moment and then chooses to take the spiral staircase, disappearing from my sight. She probably didn't want the awkwardness of waiting for the elevator in the hallway while I stared at her or tried to talk to her.

All that's left of The Little One in the hallway is the scent of her perfume and the image of her lips in my mind's eye, colored with shiny red lipstick and saying "tomorrow."

Hotel, Hallway Leading to the Elevator, Early Evening
Kate

Why did I tell him "tomorrow"? Maybe I should have stopped and listened to him for a few minutes? Listen to him now? After three days of him sending me away, not bothering to look for me, not bothering to apologize or show any interest in how I'm feeling? Now? Let him wait till tomorrow.

He took me by surprise, for a moment there I didn't know what to do, why did he surprise me like that? This isn't a good time for that, now when I'm dressed like this and already on my way. He probably came over to take his suitcase and tell me he's leaving, why do I need to think about that right now? I don't want to think about it.

Did he notice the dress I'm wearing underneath? That's not possible, it isn't visible. And the boots? Can't tell, he definitely noticed the lipstick though, he always notices when I have bold lipstick on. Why should he care about what I'm wearing if he only came over so he could take his suitcase and leave? And what's in the bag he was holding? Did he go shopping? Do you think he knows where you're going? What is he, a magician? It's not like it's written all over my forehead. It is, however, written all over my fingers, did he notice my fingers?

I walk down the street towards the metro station, unable to stop and turn back, his words continuing to echo in my head, "I'm sorry", and his image in the hallway with a book in his left hand remaining in my mind's eye.

Hotel, Room 314, Early Evening
Adam

It's taking me time to get into the room, I feel like I'm in slow-motion, as if two people exist within me, one is active and one is thinking about The Little One walking away from me down the hallway. I shut the door in slow-motion, place the book on the bed in slow-motion, walk over to the closet in slow-motion, open the closet doors in slow-motion, see that the dress and corset are gone in slow-motion, sit on the bed in slow-motion.

My thoughts have dissipated, my heart is beating slowly, I don't know whether it matters anymore if I continue to sit here, or run after her, or get up and leave, does any of it really matter? Can I even change anything at all?

"Do something," I tell myself out loud, "anything, just do something."

"Start with washing your face, one step at a time."

I walk over to the bathroom, wash my face with cold water and massage it strongly with my fingers, keeping my eyes shut. I grab a towel and notice The Little One's bra and underwear rolled up and tossed on the side by the sink, as though they were merely a worthless lump of fabric.

"Look yourself in the eyes," I command, examining the red-eyed man who is staring back at me through the dripping mirror.

"Now go find her." It doesn't really matter anymore, and it's hopeless. But you're not giving up, not now.

I slowly turn the lights off in the room, go out to the hallway, and shut the door behind me.

The Bridge, Early Evening
Adam

"Stop, Little One," I shout to her, accelerating my pace from walking to running. In the distance, on the bridge, I see The Little One leaning on the rail, a black silhouette in front of the street lamps. She doesn't look at me and I don't bother figuring out if she'd heard me and ignored me or if she hadn't heard me at all, I'm running, I want to catch up with her, put an end to this evening.

I touch her shoulder breathlessly and she turns around to look at me and I freeze.

It isn't The Little One, it's another woman, surprised by me, her eyes are red from having cried. She's looking at me with a worried and scared look. She's looking around to see if there are any other people nearby, in case she'll need to shout for help.

"I'm so sorry," I tell her once I get my breath back, hoping she understands me, "I made a mistake, I thought you were someone else, I'm so sorry," I apologize repeatedly, red with embarrassment.

She stands there looking at me, allowing a tiny smile through her tears, tightening her jacket around her body, and I stand in front of her, searching for further ways of apologizing. Now I can tell she doesn't look anything like The Little One. She's pretty, but not as pretty as my Little One. Her height is different and her lips are different and her smile is different and she actually smells like cigarettes and even the little movement she makes to wipe away her tears is different.

"It's alright," she answers me, "I was also mistaken up until now," and she grabs the suitcase next to her, backs up from the rail and walks away slowly along the bridge.

I give her a final apology, say goodbye and continue running along the path of the street lamps, thinking to myself that this woman deserved a hug, but someone else's hug.

The streets are filled with people, but not with my woman, I'm running around and looking every which way, searching for her through the crowd that passes me.

"The main thing is that you do something," I repeat to myself over and over again. I can go back to the hotel, or continue wandering the streets, or walk down to the metro, it doesn't really matter, either way I don't stand a chance in hell, but I want to feel like I did something, like I tried as much as I could, like I refused to give up on us, even if that means I have to keep searching for her all night long.

I'll start with the metro.

Metro
Kate

"What did he want to say to me? Isn't it a little too late for words? And what was that book he was holding?" The metro is less crowded now and I'm standing in the center of the carriage holding on tight in order not to fall, peering ahead as the train bends through the black tunnel. I have a few moments of silence and thoughts. "What did he want to talk to me about?" I discuss with myself, now doesn't seem like the right time for this sort of discussion, but my thoughts aren't exactly asking for my permission, they're just allowing themselves in.

"Do you think he wanted to tell you that he's leaving?" I think that's what he wanted to say. Maybe he actually wanted to tell me that he loves me and misses me? Really? After three days of not hearing from him? Suddenly he remembers? Don't be so naïve, he probably wanted to break up with me. Why did he pack his little trolley? To stay? It doesn't make sense for someone to pack a suitcase in order to stay. I need to concentrate on the stations so that I don't miss my stop, two more left.

Did he really want to apologize? It's a nice thought but it doesn't sit well with the facts and the lack of attention. One more stop and I'll get off, I think I've made enough of an effort to try and fix things, I'll think about this tomorrow, I have all of tomorrow for dealing with these thoughts. This is my stop, I need to get off now and look for the right exit, don't want to go in the wrong direction. Who did he get that book for?

Paris 8th Arrondissement, The Apartment
Kate

This looks like the right building, my palms are sweaty, probably because of the walk here, wipe them on something. A large green door with a number written over it in a rounded fashion. I glance at my black device to check the time, it's silent as usual. I'm a few minutes early, should I go in? I'll take a little stroll around the block, walk up to the street corner and back.

Walk slowly, regulate your breaths, you can't show up there all sweaty, don't want them thinking I ran all the way over here. I feel the black dress tight against my body, the stiff fabric rustles with each step I take, blending in with the sound of my heels clicking on the stone pavement. A little street, not very long, a local café at the end of it, I could stand there for a few minutes and look inside, or look over at the Eiffel Tower which is glimmering at me, I've still got time. Don't think about The Tall One and the book he was holding, check the time, I can start walking back, but slowly. I'm excited.

There, this is the entrance, check the door code that The Beauty sent you, 5546 star. Your red nails look beautiful against the number pad, the red looks almost black in the dark. Buzz, it's the right door, I don't have the wrong address. Where's the light for the stairwell? Third floor, brown door on the right, that's what she wrote me, stairs are on the right, I feel my heart pounding.

Your heels are making so much noise on the stairs, take quieter steps, it's not nice, and what if the neighbors hear you? Do you think their neighbors care? They probably know that he takes photos of women like me in high heels. The main thing is that you walk up these wooden stairs quietly.

This is the door, the brown one on the right, take a deep breath, what time is it? Calm down, everything's alright, you're at the right door at the right time and you're precisely at the right place for you.

My finger with the black lettering and the red nail is on the doorbell but I'm not thinking about it, I'm thinking about my heartbeat. I press it.

I wait for a few seconds, hearing the sound of my heart, the sound that the black dress is making as I move around in anticipation, the sound of steps on the other side of the door.

"Good evening," the photographer opens the door with a smile and hugs me politely, I smile back and hug him quickly. "Is my lipstick alright?" I ask myself, "I haven't smudged it?" I should have checked it before when I was still in the hallway.

"Come in." I follow him into the decorated living room space, light gray walls with large windows facing the now dark inner courtyard, cream-colored curtains hanging from the ceiling.

"Would you like to take your coat off?" he asks. I smile at him shyly, place my bags on the floor, take my coat off and hand it to him. He goes over to the entrance and hangs it up.

"Please, sit down," he points at the brown leather furniture. Two sofas facing each other and a modern-looking glass table between them. There are a few photography and design books on the table, one of them is open, presenting me with shiny black-and-white fashion photos.

I sit straight-backed on the edge of one of the sofas, my eyes searching for The Beauty.

"She'll probably appear down the hall soon," I think to myself and try to calm down.

"Make yourself comfortable, I'll be right back," the photographer says and disappears, I think he went to the kitchen. Where's his studio? Probably in another room.

I sit anxiously on the edge of the sofa, looking around,

scanning the room, examining the hem of my dress and my boots against the deep red Afghan carpet, trying to adjust to it all. Calm down, everything is fine, you can feel comfortable and lean back.

"Would you like some wine?" the photographer approaches me holding a bottle and two glasses. "I'm sorry," he says, "But The Beauty just told me she won't be able to make it tonight, she asked me to tell you she's sorry."

I smile at him with embarrassment and think about The Beauty and our conversations, wondering where she's disappeared to and where she is now.

"Shall we begin?" The Photographer asks me and I look away towards the open photography book on the table, staring at a photo of a model looking back at me indifferently from the glossy paper. I need to make a decision.

Alexandre III Bridge, Evening
Kate

I walk across the bridge slowly, ignoring the raindrops which have just started descending, thinking about the past evening and this whole vacation, looking at an embraced couple who are tightly holding one another. They're ignoring the rain and the few passers-by who are on their way home, they're only engaged in themselves and in their enveloping hug, as though they were in their own world.

Despite the rain, as I pass by them I slow down a bit and look at them enviously, thinking that maybe that's what we all want, that same lover who will run to us on a rainy bridge and embrace us, making us believe that love can survive and that the ending can be good, but I'm beginning to wonder whether that ending only exists in movies, and whether I should live in the world of reality. The rain gets stronger and I walk away from the embracing couple and from the bridge, careful not to slip over the wet pavement stones, thinking that my reality is an entire vacation without a single kiss. I still have a few more hours until the flight back, I need to get to the hotel and start packing.

Day Five

Hotel, Room 314, after Midnight
Adam

I put the key-card in and worriedly open the door, I'm tired, I'm wet from the rain and I think I've run out of time for searches. All those hours of wandering through the city looking for her, unable to think of anywhere specific, passing through cafés and bars and clubs, going in and coming back out and ignoring the rain.

The room is lit and I see The little One in the corner, leaning over her open suitcase, packing her clothes. When she notices me she stops and straightens up, looking at me, expecting me to say something.

I slowly approach her, feeling my legs becoming heavier with each excited and fearful step, searching for the right words to tell her, hoping so badly that she'll listen to me, that it's not too late.

"I'm sorry," I tell her. "I'm so sorry about this vacation and about how I acted during it, I'm sorry I didn't forgive you when you wanted to reconcile and I'm even more sorry for having hurt you, I'm sorry I let you leave, and most of all, I'm sorry that it took me three days to find you."

"You know," she looks at me and speaks after a few seconds, as though she's considering my words and wondering what to say. "A person can walk down the street and come across promises of a better future, and those promises are beautiful and shiny and exciting and they sparkle like a new book."

I notice the shiny black dress tossed on the floor at the entrance to the bathroom and I suddenly feel the weight of the book in my hand, as though it belongs in the past and isn't right for us anymore, as though I've missed my chance.

"And that person needs to decide," she continues, "whether to stay and cope with life, or whether to get up and follow those promises of a better future."

I want to hide the book behind my back, but she notices it and approaches me, reaching her hand out, and I have no choice but to give it to her, covered in green wrapping paper with yellow flowers, seeming so plain and pathetic to me.

"But what then?" She continues talking while turning her gaze to the book, gently unravelling the wrapping paper and leafing through it. "Do new places not have humiliations and betrayals and tears and heartaches?" and she smiles at the sight of the flower-petals dropping from between the pages and onto the bed.

"And I have made a decision," she speaks slowly, choosing her words carefully and taking another step towards me, I can smell her perfume.

"Let's go look for a café, see if anything's still open." She's really close to me now and I don't want to deliberate anymore. I lean towards her lips and kiss her, gently at first and then more firmly, enveloping her in my arms and pressing her against me, feeling her body heat and her hands caressing my neck, hesitantly at first, and then assertively, and we kiss more and more.

In the hallway, on the way to the elevator, she gives me her hand and says with a smile, "I chose you, my Tall One, you and your flower-petal books."

The End